He dropped to one knee. "I can... ...nd, Caroline. Since the first time I saw you, I have had eyes for no woman but you. You are beautiful, talented, and so pure. I know we've only known each other a few days, but I hope you'll believe me when I say I don't think I can live the rest of my life unless you're by my side. I wish we had more time, but life is far too uncertain these days. I cannot risk the chance that we'll be separated, so please say you'll do me the honor of becoming my wife."

Tears threatened to overwhelm her. "Luke." This was her dream come true. This was the fairy tale. This was the man God had created for her. And he was asking her to be his wife. He loved her! It was almost too good to be true. Yet there he was, looking up at her, the love evident on his face. How could she turn him down?

"Please say yes, Caroline."

Where she had been cold a few moments earlier, now a fire burned her skin. Luke's words had changed everything. "Yes." She nodded for emphasis. "Yes, Luke. I will marry you, as soon as we get Pa's approval."

He stood up and took her in his arms. "You've made me the happiest man alive. I want to marry you right away." He pressed a kiss on her temple.

Her toes curled, and Caroline thought she might faint. She nodded again as her eyes drifted shut. She had to be dreaming, but the man holding her felt very solid. A small voice warned her that it was too fast, but she suppressed it. She was in love with a man who loved her. What could possibly go wrong?

DIANE T. ASHLEY, a "town girl" born and raised in Mississippi, has worked more than twenty years for the House of Representatives. She rediscovered a thirst for writing, was led to a class taught by Aaron McCarver, and became a founding member of the Bards of Faith. Visit her at www.bardsoffaith.homestead.com.

AARON McCARVER is a transplanted Mississippian who was raised in the mountains near Dunlap, Tennessee. He loves his jobs of teaching at two Christian colleges and editing for Barbour Publishing. A member of ACFW, he is coauthor with Gilbert Morris of the bestselling series, The Spirit of Appalachia.

Books by Diane T. Ashley and Aaron McCarver

HEARTSONG PRESENTS

HP860—Under the Tulip Poplar
HP879—A Bouquet for Iris
HP892—The Mockingbird's Call
HP920—Across the Cotton Fields
HP943—Among the Magnolias

Don't miss out on any of our super romances. Write to us at the following address for information on our newest releases and club information.

Heartsong Presents Readers' Service
PO Box 721
Uhrichsville, OH 44683

Or visit www.heartsongpresents.com

As the River Drifts Away

Diane T. Ashley and Aaron McCarver

Heartsong Presents

To our editors extraordinaire: JoAnne Simmons and Becky Durost Fish. You are wonderful editors who have become our friends. Thanks for giving wings to our dreams. We deeply appreciate the work you put into improving our stories. And for everyone else who wants you to edit their books. . .we call dibs!

A note from the Authors:
We love to hear from our readers! You may correspond with us by writing:

Diane T. Ashley and Aaron McCarver
Author Relations
PO Box 721
Uhrichsville, OH 44683

ISBN 978-1-61626-371-3

AS THE RIVER DRIFTS AWAY

Copyright © 2011 by Diane T. Ashley and Aaron McCarver. All rights reserved. Except for use in any review, the reproduction or utilization of this work in whole or in part in any form by any electronic, mechanical, or other means, now known or hereafter invented, is forbidden without the permission of Heartsong Presents, an imprint of Barbour Publishing, Inc., PO Box 721, Uhrichsville, Ohio 44683.

All scripture quotations are taken from the King James Version of the Bible.

All of the characters and events in this book are fictitious. Any resemblance to actual persons, living or dead, or to actual events is purely coincidental.

Our mission is to publish and distribute inspirational products offering exceptional value and biblical encouragement to the masses.

PRINTED IN THE U.S.A.

one

"Abigail, I'm not planning to take you and the girls with me this time." Pa straightened and dusted his hands after tossing a fresh log on the fire. "It's far too dangerous for gadding about."

Ma sighed and pulled her shawl closer about her shoulders. "We're not talking about going on a sightseeing trip, Nathan. And you'll be there to protect us."

Caroline Pierce studied the grooves in the pine floor, wishing she could think of something to say that would bring her parents to agreement. She was eighteen years old, after all. Old enough to find the right words. "Perhaps we sh. . . shouldn't go to Vicksburg." She could feel the pressure of her parents' gazes but refused to look up. Her heart beat a rapid tattoo. Why had she decided to voice her opinion?

"Don't be nonsensical, dearest." Ma reached past the arm of the sofa and patted her knee. "You're not afraid, are you? We'll be much safer with your father than staying here in Jackson all alone."

Ma's tone was gentle, so why couldn't Caroline calm the beating of her heart? She loved her mother and ought to be accustomed to her outspokenness. But she wished just this once that Ma would quietly accept Pa's pronouncement. Then they could turn their attention to some other subject, like yesterday's sermon. She would even welcome a discussion on

5

what color to paint the parlor or whether or not she could mend the tear in her counterpane.

The fireplace logs shifted, and heat from the dancing flames brushed her cheeks. A deep breath seemed to steady her nerves somewhat. Wondering if she'd lost her mind, Caroline opened her mouth to answer. "I'm sorry to disagree with you, Ma. Pa would not make such a decision lightly. We have a duty to listen to him."

"You're quite right, Caroline." Ma's eyes crinkled at the corners as she smiled. "But that does not preclude my discussing the matter with him. Or with you either."

Her hands twisted in her lap. Caroline did not want to "discuss" things. She had already expressed her opinion. But she did not have the courage to argue with her strong-willed parent. Why not accept Pa's bidding? It would make life much easier, and much quieter, in the Pierce home. But Ma was not likely to change, so Caroline folded her lips and remained silent while wondering why they couldn't just go along with Pa. He deserved their respectful acceptance of his decisions.

"If your mother did not challenge me, I'd be certain she was ill." Her father settled on the sofa and placed an arm around her mother's shoulders. "I've never been under any illusion about her timidity."

Caroline wondered if she would ever understand others in her family. Was she a changeling? But that wasn't possible. Even she could see how much she looked like her father. Both of them had blond hair, fair skin, and eyes as blue as a summer sky. But at three inches above five feet, she had not inherited her father's height.

Pa was a well-respected pastor at one of the largest churches in town, but at home he often bowed to the wishes of his wife. Ma and even Tory, Caroline's younger sister, seemed to take delight in disputing many of his decisions.

Perhaps I am the odd one. They didn't suffer from the same malady that twisted Caroline's tongue in knots every time she tried to speak. She nodded and dipped her head once more.

The door to the study opened, and she glanced up to see Tory rushing through the door. Her sister's dark hair fell in thick waves about her shoulders, and excitement brought extra beauty to her face. Grandma said Tory looked like she had when she was younger.

Tory would soon be collecting men's hearts the way some young women collected flowers. Although she was a full four years younger than Caroline, she was already turning heads at church. She was definitely the most beautiful member of the family and the liveliest. But it was her innate kindness that made her irresistible to young people of both sexes. If a group of youngsters was gathered together, Tory was almost certain to be at its center.

"Come quickly." Tory clasped her hands in front of her chest. "A group of soldiers is marching down the street. You have to see them. They are so handsome in their gray uniforms."

"Please tell me you have not been ogling the young men." Pa's sigh was audible.

Ma rose from the sofa. "I'm sure she's done no such thing." Her dark-brown gaze held the same warning as her voice. "Have you, Tory?"

"Of course not." Tory's wide skirts twisted as she turned toward the door to the hallway. "Come along, Caroline. Hurry, or you'll miss them."

Pa stood and offered his arm to Ma. Caroline followed them to the hallway, a smile turning up the corners of her mouth as Pa placed a quick kiss on Ma's cheek. Her love for him was clear in the gaze Ma trained on him as they walked out. Was their love for each other the reason for Pa's tolerance? Caroline worried at the question as her sister flung the front doors wide and a blast of frigid air rushed into the hallway.

"Brr." Her mother's shoulders lifted as the cold surrounded them. "Wait until we've put on our wraps."

"Sorry." Her younger sister closed the doors, a penitent look on her face.

"You allow yourself to get far too excited, Tory." Her mother took her cloak from a hook on the wall. "If you wish to be included in adult gatherings, you'll have to temper your actions with the same good sense your older sister displays."

Caroline felt another blush as she accepted her green wool cloak from her father and wrapped it around her shoulders. She was not comfortable being held up as an example. She had far too many faults.

"I believe we are ready to brave the cold." Pa nodded at Tory. "Let's see these soldiers of yours."

This time when she opened the doors, Tory managed it with a bit more grace. But as Caroline crossed the threshold, her incorrigible sister winked at her, and a giggle threatened to escape. A prime example of why she should not be held up as a model of good behavior.

The street was alive with marching men. Her gaze widened as she stepped to the rail surrounding the deep porch. "Oh my."

Tory grabbed her arm. "Aren't they marvelous?"

A frown brought Caroline's brows together. Marching in formation, five abreast, the sea of gray slouch caps and uniforms filled the dirt road from edge to edge. But as she looked closer, she realized their uniforms were tattered and faded. Sadness and empathy filled her. "Where are they going?"

"Probably to Canton." Her father pointed to the north. "President Davis has ordered General Johnston to keep the Jackson area safe as well as lend support to General Pemberton's troops in Vicksburg."

"Some of them look so young." Ma shook her head. "Younger than you are, Tory. It makes me sad to think of the boys who won't be alive when this war is over."

Tory had leaned over the edge of the rail, but she straightened and looked toward her parents. "Don't say such a terrible thing. Amy Parsons says the South is winning the war. Maybe all our boys will come back unhurt."

Caroline found herself agreeing with her mother. The war had gone on for several years now. Hopes for a quick end had faded as the battles continued to rage, and every day they heard of families who had lost sons, brothers, or fathers.

Pa shook his head. "No matter which side wins, war is a terrible thing. Especially this war between states. I've read in the local newspapers of brothers joining opposite sides and meeting each other on the battlefield."

Caroline's jaw tightened. She hated the idea of siblings as enemies. "We should pray for them." She reached for her father's hand. "And for a quick end to the war."

⁂

The first thing Caroline noticed as she disembarked from the carriage was a huge, conical pipe mounted on the nose of a boxy, open-windowed conveyance. The black smoke belching from the pipe drifted back over the roofs of cargo and passenger cars. "Is that the train we'll be taking?"

Her father nodded and pulled out his pocket watch. "We should be leaving the station within an hour."

"There's another train." Tory stepped up beside her and pointed to a second engine pointed south. "How can you tell which one we should board?"

"That one is going to New Orleans." Pa put away his watch and held out his arm for Ma. "Stay with us, you two. I don't want to have to come looking for you."

Picking up her skirt, Caroline picked her way around bales, barrels, and boxes. She almost fell when an obnoxious businessman pushed past her and was only saved from ending up facedown in a puddle by the quick reflexes of a nearby soldier.

"Careful, ma'am." His hand gripped her arm.

Her breath got stuck in her throat, but Caroline managed to mumble her thanks. He bowed and was quickly lost in the crowd.

"He was handsome." Tory's familiar voice restored her equilibrium.

Caroline rolled her eyes. "You think every man above the age of ten is handsome, especially if he's wearing a uniform."

Tory stuck out her tongue.

"Careful or your expression may get stuck that way." Caroline repeated the warning their mother had often used when she was younger.

"Come along, girls." Ma's voice stopped Tory from answering.

They waited a few feet back as their father spoke briefly with the conductor. Nearby, a farmer made arrangements for livestock to be delivered to his home, his voice sharp as he directed the loading onto a wagon.

"Did you see the size of the lantern on the front of the locomotive?" Tory's voice held a note of awe. "It's almost as large as my bedroom window."

"Yes." Caroline looked toward the large engine. "It must be nearly as bright as moonlight."

Tory nodded. "I wonder why they need it though. That large shovel on the front of the train looks as though it would sweep away any obstacles."

"I've read of Union soldiers pulling up tracks and causing Confederate trains to have wrecks. Perhaps they need the lantern to make sure the track ahead has not been destroyed."

"You young ladies don't have to worry about a thing." The conductor, a tall man with a kindly smile, walked over to them. His reddish-blond hair reminded her of Grandpa back in Natchez. "We'll have you safely to your destination before nightfall."

Tory's face fell, but all Caroline felt was relief at the man's reassurance. She could never be as daring as her younger sister. The conductor indicated the steps with a broad gesture, and she turned to realize their parents had already boarded the train.

She climbed the steps and entered the cabin, feeling her stomach curdle as the floor pitched slightly under the movements of the other travelers. She swallowed hard and moved forward, looking for some sign of her parents. How had they gotten separated so quickly?

"There they are." Tory pointed to a seat at the back, and Caroline breathed a sigh of relief as she recognized them. Ma was already seated next to the window, but Pa was removing his coat and hat. At least he had not begun looking for them.

Tory and Caroline settled themselves on the seat in front of their parents. Tory looked out the window and pointed to a man who was carrying their trunks on his shoulders. "I do hope he doesn't drop my trunk. I cannot imagine how embarrassing it would be to have all my clothing scattered on the ground."

"You have such an imagination." Caroline sometimes wished she had inherited a small portion of Tory's zest for life. . .as well as a large helping of her outspokenness. She sighed and folded her hands in her lap. It was not as though she found life difficult, and she knew the good Lord had created her to have her own strengths, but it would be nice to take pleasure in each day with the wholehearted joy her sister displayed.

Tory continued to remark on all the things that caught her attention as the car filled with passengers. The ring of a brass bell somewhere ahead brought the conductor past them, stopping here or there to help people stow their bags and cloaks.

The train shuddered, and she gripped the edge of her seat, her heart tripping. Caroline twisted her head toward the window and saw the depot moving backward.

Beside her, Tory clapped her hands together. "We're moving."

A second glance out the window proved her sister right. The train, not the depot, was moving, picking up speed with every turn of the metal wheels beneath them. She pried her fingers from the edge of the wooden bench and placed them in her lap once more. Taking a deep breath, she forced a smile to her lips. "So we are."

Tory didn't seem to notice her discomfort, so enthralled was she by the passing scenery. "I wonder if we'll see any Yankees."

"I doubt it." Pa's voice came from the seat behind them. "And I thought I told you not to use that term. You can call them Union or Federal soldiers, but you will be punished if I hear you use that vulgar term again."

"Yes, sir." Tory's voice was penitent.

Caroline hated to see the sheen of tears in her sister's eyes. She reached over and gave Tory's hand a squeeze.

Tory rewarded her with a wobbly smile.

"Look at all the smoke." Caroline indicated the black swirls coming from the engine at the front of the train. "Thankfully it's cool enough in here so that we can keep the windows shut."

While Tory watched the passing scenery, Caroline pulled needlework from her reticule and began stitching. "I don't know how you have such patience." Tory's whisper raised a smile. "And your stitches are so much finer than mine. You will make an excellent wife for some handsome soldier."

Color heated Caroline's cheeks. "Don't be silly. I don't even have a suitor. I'm sure you will marry before anyone makes me an offer."

Tory made a choked sound. "Anyone who gets to know you will never be able to resist your sweetness and feminine abilities. You are the perfect example of the good wife Solomon talks about in the Bible. Why, who knows? He could even be here on this train and watching you sitting here demurely with your stitchery in your lap. He's probably trying to figure out who you are and how to arrange an introduction."

This time the choked sound came from Caroline's throat. "You are being a silly goose." But her heart stumbled. Was it true? She looked around at the passengers she could see. A short, overweight businessman in the seat opposite them had tipped his hat over his face and was apparently sleeping. Up ahead she could see a passably handsome man sitting next to his beautiful wife. A pair of soldiers were laughing and talking as though they had no thought of war or death. Tory's imagination was as vivid as ever but had no basis in reality.

She returned her attention to her needlework. Only God knew what was in store, but she had no doubt He had a bright future in mind for both her and her sister.

two

Luke Talbot sawed at the tough slice of beef and wished for the time before the war, the days when good meat was readily available at restaurants. The days when he could expect a decent meal to complement the beautiful young lady seated opposite him. Why had he let Gram talk him into coming to Vicksburg, anyway?

For a wife.

He glanced toward Marianna Lister, the young lady sitting across from him. Glossy black hair framed her beautiful face. Miss Lister's complexion was flawless, as was her genteel conversation and fashionable attire. Yet when he compared her to the woman who had stolen his heart and then betrayed it—

Luke shook his head to stop that train of thought. No need to compare her to Amelia Montgomery. No female would ever outshine her memory. Even though Amelia's lies and subterfuges had probably cost him his chance to become a general in the Confederate army, she would always be the first woman he'd ever loved. It didn't matter that she had betrayed the South and then had the effrontery to choose Jared Stuart instead of him; Amelia had claimed the better part of Luke's heart.

"It is so delightful to spend an evening away from my family." Miss Lister ignored the meat on her plate and nibbled at a biscuit. "Papa always drones on and on about the war. It scares my poor mother half to death. You would think Yankees were standing on our very doorstep if you listened to him."

"Your father is probably right to be concerned." Luke finally managed to separate a bite of meat from the serving on his plate. "Lincoln has made it very plain he would love to capture the city of Vicksburg."

Marianna dabbed at her mouth with her napkin. "That may be so, but it's most unlikely. General Grant will soon realize he cannot prevail and will leave us alone. He's already tried three times to take the city, but our troops have outwitted him at every turn."

"I have the feeling the general is not yet ready to admit defeat."

"Let him come." The young lady opposite him raised her chin in a defiant gesture. "I refuse to cower like some child who is afraid of an imaginary hobgoblin."

Luke smiled. He had to admire the young lady's courage. In fact, there was much to admire about Miss Lister. A very fine example of a true Southern belle, Marianna was beautiful and intelligent. She was also proving herself to be an entertaining companion. She was the best of the crop his grandmother had paraded in front of him since his arrival in Mississippi before Christmas.

"I can almost see you running off a whole platoon of Yankees with a broom and a parasol."

"I suppose you're making a joke at my expense. But I'll do whatever is necessary to protect my home and family."

"Pardon me, Miss Lister." Luke hid his smile. He hadn't meant to insult her. "I didn't mean to make light of your words. I have no doubt you would do a wonderful job of running those Yankees off. I only wish the ladies back in Tennessee had half of your fervor. When we men go off to fight, it's comforting to know we've left our homes in the capable, courageous hands of ladies such as yourself."

Her smile was as wide as the Mississippi River and as

bright as sunlight. He ought to tell her that, but he didn't want to rush into anything. There would be time for him to get to know Miss Lister better before he began spouting effusive compliments. Instead he satisfied himself with returning her attractive smile.

Luke reached for his goblet of water at the same time she did, and their knuckles brushed. Her eyes widened slightly in surprise, and a faint flush colored her cheeks. In that moment, he thought he might be able to bury his feelings for Amelia after all. Perhaps Marianna Lister could fill the hole Amelia had left behind.

As their dinner continued, he discovered Marianna's talents ranged from music to watercolors. She also volunteered with the Southern Ladies Relief Society, where she distributed tracts to wounded soldiers. Of course, she also found time to attend balls and visit friends. On Sundays, she worshipped at a local church, and she even rolled bandages for the local hospital on Sunday afternoons.

"I don't know how you do it, Miss Lister." Luke put his fork down next to his empty plate and signaled the waiter to bring the bill. "How do you ever find time for your beauty rest?"

"It's not difficult. I find sufficient time, especially now that the war has curtailed many of the social engagements we would normally enjoy. Mother says it is a shame I have come of age during this beastly war. The good Lord knows there are not many eligible men anymore. It's one reason I was so happy when your grandmother wrote to us of your arrival."

Luke was in the process of pulling money out of his pocketbook so he concentrated on that rather than the feeling of being pursued by an experienced hunter. The material of his shirt rubbed at the back of his neck, but he refused to give in to the instinct to scratch it. He ought to realize by now that until he married he would be the target of matchmaking mamas and their eager daughters. He was young, wealthy, and passably good looking. But he could not remember any young lady ever being quite so forthcoming about her goals. He supposed it must be a cultural difference.

He would have to remember to ask Hampton Boothe about it the next time he saw his friend. Hampton had been a fount of information about the mores of the local society, and he could likely tell Luke whether Miss Lister was ingenuous or predatory. "I see."

The waiter approached the table once again, and Luke handed him several Confederate bills. The man counted the bills and bowed. "Thank you, sir. I hope you will return to dine with us again soon."

Luke nodded, but his stomach clenched at the thought of fighting to slice his way through another piece of meat that had more in common with jerked beef than roast beef. Unless the other eating establishments in Vicksburg had equally poor offerings, he doubted he would be returning any time soon.

He gathered their wraps and escorted Miss Lister to his carriage, tucking a thick fur around her ankles before sitting across from her in the carriage and signaling to the driver they were ready to leave.

The clang of a train's bell made her lean forward and pull back the velvet curtain covering the coach window. "Do you think we could go to the station and watch the people disembark?"

Luke cast a dubious glance at the gathering dusk. "Won't your parents be expecting you to return home soon?"

"I suppose so." Her lips puckered slightly in a charming pout.

Feeling a bit like a heel for denying her request, Luke

crossed his arms over his chest. "Perhaps I could escort you to the station in the future when we have more time."

"Could we?" The pout melted into a warm smile. "You are very kind. I know you must think it odd of me, but I enjoy watching people. Their faces inspire my paintings."

"I would consider it my pleasure." The carriage halted, and he found himself torn by conflicting emotions. He felt a desire to please her, make her continue to smile at him in that admiring way. But his conscience warned him to maintain a proper distance or find himself cornered into proposing to her before he knew for certain whether she would make a proper wife.

So he escorted her to the front door and handed her over to the butler with a promise to call on her again soon. Then he made his escape into his carriage. All the way back to the hotel, he thought about the time he'd spent with Marianna. But would she be the right choice to become Mrs. Luke Talbot?

❧

"I'm so glad you agreed to escort me to church, Luke." His grandmother took his hand as she stepped out of the carriage. "I was afraid you might have other plans this evening. . .like visiting with the breathtaking Marianna Lister."

"Not at all. I wouldn't dream of putting another lady ahead of you."

She swatted his arm. "Flatterer. I'm not blind, you know. You've spent nearly every waking hour at her parents' home this week, culminating in your dinner together. You must know the whole town is abuzz with talk of romance."

"You shouldn't listen to gossip, Grandma." He held out his elbow and waited until she grasped it before moving toward the wide church doors. "Besides, you've been talking about the fiery Brother Pierce almost since the day I arrived at

Shady Oaks. I am most anxious to hear his learned sermon."

A giggle turned his head to the right where a pair of young women stood whispering to each other. Rays of the setting sun gilded the blond hair of the taller one. She had an arresting face—it spoke to him of sweetness and a shy personality. Her companion had dark hair and a much livelier expression, bringing to mind some of the escapades he'd been involved in when he was a young boy.

The darker one leaned up and whispered something while looking directly at him. He had no idea what she said, but whatever it was caused the willowy, blond girl's cheeks to suffuse with bright color. Her eyes, as blue as the lakes back home, widened when their gazes met, and her mouth formed a perfect *O* of surprise.

An instant later he was past them, entering the candlelit sanctuary with his grandmother still on his arm. He wanted nothing more than to turn around, go back outside, and introduce himself to the beautiful blond. But he knew he could not. He had a duty to fulfill to his relative. Good manners and good sense made him move forward. He found a seat for them on a half-empty pew and helped his grandmother get comfortable. As soon as he was seated, he twisted around to see if the girl had entered the room.

"Are you looking for Miss Lister?" Grandma's voice brought him back to reality with a thump.

What was he thinking? That he wanted to meet another young lady? She was probably engaged, maybe even married. The idea tightened his chest. She could not be. She was far too innocent. He almost laughed out loud at the thought. How could he possibly know that? He'd not spoken a single word to her. Yet something inside him knew.

"No. I. . .uh. . .I. . ." He tried to gather his thoughts. He could feel his grandmother's gaze on his face. "Do you know the two girls who were standing outside as we entered the church?"

The question in her eyes turned to confusion. "What girls?"

"Didn't you see them? One was a raven-haired lady, girl really. But it was her friend I would really like to meet. Her hair was as bright as sunlight, golden as a field of wheat. She is one of the most striking women I have ever seen."

Grandma looked back over her shoulder, nodding to someone she knew. "I don't know who you're talking about, Luke. I don't see anyone matching your description."

"They'll have to come inside. Why else would they be loitering about the entrance to the church?"

His grandmother shrugged and turned her attention back to the front of the room. "We're bound to see them sooner or later."

Hoping her words were prophetic, Luke straightened and pulled on the sleeves of his frock coat. The dark wool was warm enough, but since the church was heated, he was beginning to wish he'd chosen something a little less scratchy.

Marianna Lister and her family arrived, but the pew he and his grandmother occupied was already crowded, so they spoke briefly before procuring a pew closer to the front.

The pianist struck a chord, and a tall man, accompanied by his wife and family, walked down the aisle to the front of the church. Luke's attention was first centered on the man, who had to be Nathan Pierce. Why did he look so familiar? His gaze fell on the pastor's children, and recognition dawned. The beautiful blond girl. She was the pastor's daughter. Miss Pierce. He settled against the back of the pew. As soon as the sermon was over, he would make sure they were introduced.

Brother Pierce stepped up to the pulpit and opened his Bible. "I'm glad to see so many here this evening. As I look out on all of you, I see some who are hurting, some who are lost, and some who are simply counting the minutes until I am done speaking."

Guilt straightened Luke's spine. He was not here to meet females, no matter how alluring they were. He had come to hear a man share his insight about the heart and mind of God.

" 'Blessed are the poor in spirit: for theirs is the kingdom of heaven.' " The pastor lifted his hands above the pulpit. "This is the promise of Jesus for all of us. But what good does that do me today, Pastor? The kingdom of heaven is not here. I am hurting. I am lost. I don't know how I'm going to survive the pain."

Luke was disappointed. Was this the man who had such a mighty reputation? He should have known the message would be useless. He was not hurt or lost. He was young and strong, and he knew exactly what he was doing. He'd come to Mississippi to help his grandmother keep Shady Oaks running after Grandpa's death. He'd been transferred from Knoxville at his father's request due to the questions surrounding the arrest and escape of a known Union traitor, the notorious Mockingbird.

A sigh filled him once more for the trouble he'd experienced because of Amelia Montgomery's wrongheadedness. If only he'd realized what trouble she would cause him, he never would have allowed himself to become involved in her life.

He glanced at his grandmother from the corner of his eye. She was completely immersed in what the pastor was saying, so he returned to contemplation of his past. Luke's life may have taken some unexpected twists and turns, but he had no doubt he was on the right road. God willing, he would still have a chance to serve the Confederacy and achieve a respectable rank before this war was over. And he would find the right girl to marry, someone whose beliefs were more in line with his own, someone like Marianna Lister.

A smile touched his lips. In a few years, he would be as successful as he'd always dreamed. He would have a house full of children, an adoring wife, and a thriving sugarcane plantation. He would probably have earned several battlefield promotions. Who knew? He might even attain the rank of general one day. No, this sermon had absolutely nothing to do with him.

Luke's attention was brought back to the church service by the sound of women's voices singing "O Worship the King." He glanced toward the pulpit and saw the two girls he'd noticed before. Their voices harmonized, weaving in and out to form a tapestry of images in his mind. He sat enthralled by the performance, saddened when they reached the last note. For a moment, nothing but silence filled the large room, as though all in the congregation were holding their breath.

When Brother Pierce once again took the podium, he bowed his head and spoke in low tones, exhorting God for a quick end to the war and suffering. He mentioned several families by name who had lost fathers, sons, or brothers to the fighting. He went on to call on God to bless those who were far from home, men on both sides of the battle.

Luke felt his shoulders tighten. Should the man be praying for the enemy? It didn't seem right to him. The pastor ought to limit his supplications to the Confederate soldiers. He raised his head and looked around. No one else seemed particularly concerned at the prayer, so he closed his eyes once again and counted to fifty while waiting for the man to utter *Amen*. Luke stood immediately and held out his hand to his grandmother.

"You'll have to wait a minute. These old bones don't move as well as they used to." She gathered her cloak and reticule and leaned forward.

He reached down to help her rise. "Let me help you."

"What's the matter? Is there a fire outside?"

Feeling like a corrected youngster, Luke held his tongue. But he couldn't quite keep his sigh inside his chest.

"Oh, all right." She twisted her arm away from him and grasped the pew in front of her. "I'm coming."

The other churchgoers were now crowding the center aisle, greeting each other and discussing the sermon, the war, or whatever other subject came to mind. Luke would have liked to avoid getting stuck, but it was too late to worry about it now.

"Mr. Talbot, there you are." A hand touched his shoulder.

Luke's frown became a smile as he realized Miss Lister was standing behind him. Perhaps his grandmother's slowness was for the best after all. "Hello. I saw you come in with your family."

"Did you enjoy the sermon?"

What could he say? Did he dare tell a lie in God's house? Would he be struck by lightning? Paralysis? "I know his words must have been comforting for those who have lost loved ones." He was pleased with the answer. It was not a lie. In fact he had no doubt that many of the people here had been touched by the man's words. Just not him.

"Yes, I thought so, too." She gazed up at him, her hazel eyes showing admiration and hope. Her gaze moved past him. "Good evening, Mrs. Darby. Did you enjoy the sermon, too?"

"Of course I did." She cleared her throat. "Brother Pierce is a talented speaker with a prodigious understanding of the Bible. I hope to hear him again before he returns to his church in Jackson."

Miss Lister's parents caught up with them then, and the conversation turned general. Finally they began to move to the front of the church. But Luke's sense of urgency faded away. He doubted he'd get the chance to be introduced to the lovely blond singer. Not while Miss Lister was hanging on his every word.

The pastor was still greeting members of the congregation and receiving their compliments. He was flanked on one side by his wife, an auburn-haired woman whom Luke would describe as striking rather than beautiful. On the pastor's far side stood the two girls. Once again Luke's gaze clashed with that of the blond. What was it about her that drew his attention? Her cheeks reddened, and she looked down toward her feet.

Grandma must have realized something had happened. Her gaze swiveled from him to the pastor's daughter, and her lips tightened into a thin, straight line. "It's time for us to get back to the hotel, Grandson. Say good night to Marianna and her parents." Her grip on his arm tightened enough to resemble a pinch as she stepped past the preacher and his family with a nod. "Words to live by, Pastor." The woman who'd been so slow inside the church practically pulled Luke down the steps to the waiting carriage.

"Good night, Mrs. Darby, Captain Talbot." He heard the wistful note in Marianna's voice and turned to bow to her.

She was standing on the bottom step, directly in front of the blond he'd wanted to meet. Marianna was all poise and sophistication, exactly the type of girl he'd always thought he would one day marry. But next to the simple, self-effacing young lady whose name he had yet to learn, Marianna seemed too polished—almost an imitation of what a real lady should be.

"Come along, Luke." His grandmother's querulous tones pulled him out of his thoughts. She looked out from the carriage and waved to Marianna's mother. "I assume we'll see you at the Lancasters' ball, Georgia."

"Of course," Mrs. Lister answered her. "We wouldn't miss such an important gathering. Dare I hope to see you and Captain Talbot there?"

"I imagine so." Grandma leaned back against the seat. "We'll be here all week to hear Brother Pierce, so there's no reason for us to miss the biggest ball of the new year."

Their attendance was news to Luke, but he supposed he shouldn't mind. It would give him a chance to see all the single young women that Vicksburg had to offer, perhaps even the girl he had missed meeting this evening.

As the driver pulled away from the curb, Luke caught one more glimpse of her. She was looking away from him as though he had not made nearly the impression on her that she had made on him. He could not believe it. Not that he was particularly vain. But females usually fell over themselves to draw his attention. He was definitely going to have to visit the pastor's shy daughter.

three

"Ma, did you see that man who was looking at me and Caroline?"

"It's 'Caroline and me,' Tory. I wonder if you learned anything from that private tutor in Jackson." Caroline's mother shook out her napkin before placing it in her lap. "No, I did not see anyone looking at either of you, but then the church was rather crowded."

Caroline took a bowl of creamed potatoes from her father and put some on her plate before handing them off to her younger sister. She bent a warning frown at Tory and shook her head slightly. Casting about for a change of subject, she cleared her throat and turned her attention to her father. "It was crowded because of Pa's sermon."

"I don't know about that." Her father smiled at her. "But what is this about a young man ogling you? Did you notice anything odd?"

The temptation to say no was very strong, but Caroline knew she could not lie. "I wouldn't say odd, but I did see a man who seemed to enjoy our duet."

Tory rolled her eyes. "A very handsome man and very well dressed. He was tall, with flashing black eyes and a mustache. I first noticed him while we were standing out in front of the church. He was escorting an older lady, probably his mother, but he couldn't take his eyes off of us."

A wave of heat rushed up and burned Caroline's cheeks. "I don't know about that."

"Why shouldn't a young man be interested in you?" Ma

took a steaming biscuit from a cloth-covered bowl and reached for the dish of butter. "You are beautiful, poised, and talented. The only reason you don't have a bevy of suitors is because your father and I have not been very diligent about attending social occasions. But that is about to change." She glanced toward Pa, who nodded his encouragement. "Your father has received an invitation to a ball at the home of Mr. and Mrs. Lancaster this coming Friday, and we have decided to attend. Of course you will join us."

Caroline's mouth dropped open. A ball? "But you know I don't like those ostentatious parties."

"I'll go with you, Ma." Tory was so excited her voice came out with a squeak.

Pa shook his head. "You're too young to go to a ball. Don't be so anxious to grow up."

A pout replaced Tory's hopeful expression. "It's not fair."

"I'll tell you every detail." Caroline sympathized with her sister's disappointment even though she would have gladly stayed home and let Tory go in her place. "Everything from the decorations to the gowns to the music. You'll feel like you were there with me."

"It won't be the same, though." Tory sat back in her chair, crossed her arms over her chest, and sighed loudly.

"You will get your turn in a few short years." Ma's voice was pragmatic. "As your pa says, you should not be so anxious to take on the responsibilities of adulthood."

Caroline pushed her plate away. "I don't know why anyone wants to have a ball right now anyway. Don't they realize we're at war?"

"Yes, dear." Ma reached for the salt cellar. "It's an attempt to ignore the truth."

Picking up a serving dish of sliced roast, Pa nodded his agreement. "We know things are not going well for the

Confederacy. The only hope they ever had was that the North would allow secession after a few token battles. But that has not been the case. The longer the fighting continues, the less likely the South will emerge victorious."

Silence fell as they considered his words. Caroline wished the Confederate leaders understood the situation as clearly as Pa did so they would negotiate a surrender before the death toll rose even higher. How many more families had to lose loved ones before the war was brought to an end?

Ma cleared her throat. "I'll need the carriage for an hour or so tomorrow, Nathan. We are almost completely out of sugar and flour. And we'll need to see if we can find any lace to spruce up Caroline's blue dress."

She allowed her mind to wander as her parents worked out the details of their shopping excursion. Maybe they would even see the stranger from church while they were at the market. Butterflies tickled her stomach at the thought. He was so handsome and as tall as Pa. Her head would probably fit under his chin.

A shiver made its way down her spine as she remembered his pitch-black eyes and the distinguished side-whiskers that gave him an air of authority. The embodiment of every hero she'd ever dreamed of meeting, he might have stepped directly from the pages of a romance novel.

She might not have formally met him, but Caroline felt like she knew so much about the man. He cared about family as evidenced by his escort of his relative. His presence at Pa's service proved he was a man of faith. She had no doubt he was a man she could lean on, someone on whom she could rely, someone who would take care of her and protect her from all harm.

But what was she thinking? Caroline could never draw the admiration of such a hero. He had probably been looking at Tory, the real beauty of the family. Gloom and doubt gathered around her shoulders. Besides, hadn't he been talking to another young lady right before he left? He hadn't made the slightest attempt to introduce himself to her parents, the first step he would have to take if he was interested in meeting her.

Notwithstanding Tory's opinion, it was obvious he had not been attracted to either of them. What did it matter anyway? It was unlikely she'd ever see him again. And if she did, she'd probably discover that he was nothing like she imagined.

He may have already left the city, returning to his home or even to a stint with the army. Her heart thudded against her chest at the thought of his riding into danger.

"Caroline, have you fallen asleep at the table?" Her mother's voice interrupted her melancholy thoughts.

She looked around to find she was the center of attention. "I'm sorry. I guess my attention wandered."

Pa chuckled. "I believe she may be dreaming of Friday's party."

Caroline would have disagreed, but then she would've had to explain what she had been dreaming of. . .or rather whom. So she glanced down at her lap and said nothing at all.

"I cannot wait until I get to be eighteen."

Glad her sister's statement had drawn their parents' attention, Caroline stood and began stacking the plates to take to the kitchen. "You'll be much better at this than I ever will."

Tory picked up the napkins while Ma gathered the silverware. "I don't know why you shouldn't be the center of attention on Friday."

Caroline couldn't imagine an eventuality more frightening than the image her mother's words conjured. The only way she'd ever become the center of attention would be if she did something incredibly clumsy, like trip on the dance floor or spill punch down the front of her dress.

Dread filled her as she carried the dishes to the kitchen. She could only hope her mother's words were not prophetic.

❧

"You need to get over the girl who broke your heart, Luke." Grandma's voice penetrated the dark cloud around him.

Luke turned to her. "How did you know?"

He felt cold and exposed even though it was warm enough in their private sitting room. The homey sound and smell of a crackling fire filled the room.

Grandma smirked. "It's not very hard to figure out what's going on in that thick head of yours. It's the same thing that goes on in any man's head when a woman has spurned him. But I'm saying this from the wealth of my experience—no woman is worth spending your time mooning over her."

A thought burst into his head with the suddenness of a lightning bolt. "That's really why we came to town, isn't it?"

His grandmother had been looping thread into an intricate weave she called crochet, but now she put the handwork in her lap. "Nonsense. We came because I wanted to hear Nathan Pierce preach. Surely you've seen the flyers posted all over town." She waited for his nod. "One was delivered to me at Shady Oaks. It piqued my interest. So I thought it would be a good idea for both of us to come to Vicksburg. It's as simple as that."

He cocked an eyebrow. Somehow her explanation was a little too glib to be believable. "And my parents didn't write to you about my recent betrothal?"

She tried to hold his gaze, but her eyelids fluttered. She looked down and reached for the hooked needle and yarn. "They might have mentioned something about a girl from back home. But they said you were better off without her."

As he had expected. "So which of you came up with the idea of finding me a wife? I doubt it was Pa."

"Your parents want you to be happy, Luke." Her fingers poked the needle and twisted it deftly. "And so do I."

"What about what I want?" He blew out a disgusted breath. "Did either you or my mother consider the fact that I will most likely be called back into battle? What do you expect me to do? Abandon a new bride on our wedding night?"

"Of course not." She glanced up at him for a moment before concentrating on her hands once more. "No one knows what is going to happen with this war. Perhaps you won't even have to face those Yanks. Perhaps they'll give up and go away."

Luke pushed himself up from his chair and walked to the fireplace. "You cannot believe such drivel. The Unionists are desperate to control the Mississippi River, and capturing Vicksburg will secure their goal. I met with Colonel Autrey this morning. He informed me of a large contingent of enemy soldiers apparently led by General Grant that is still bivouacked only a few dozen miles on the other side of the Mississippi. As soon as the weather allows, they'll probably march on this very town. Pemberton is going to need all the men he can muster. War is coming here sooner rather than later."

"You may be right, but it is not here today, nor is it likely to arrive before the end of the week. Only God is in control of the future. All we can do is work our way through today."

He pushed the toe of his boot against the stack of dry wood to one side of the fireplace. "Exactly what work do you have planned for today?"

Grandma placed her needlework into a basket beside her. "I thought we might pay a visit on the Listers. You and Marianna seem to be getting along fairly well."

"She is a sweet girl." He turned and caught the smile on

his grandmother's face. "But don't go posting any notices in the paper yet. I am not ready to declare my interest in her."

"You ought not wait too long, Grandson. Someone will soon snap up a prize like that young lady. She is talented, kind, and quite beautiful. Her family is well received in this area. She would be an excellent choice for you."

"You are partial to her because you are friends with her mother."

"I admit to a certain amount of partiality." Grandma rang for a servant. "But if she were not a good match for you, no amount of friendship with any of her family would sway my opinion."

A quiet knock on the door interrupted their conversation. When his grandmother called for the person to enter, Luke listened while she gave the servant instructions for a carriage to take them on their outing. He was not deeply averse to the idea of finding a bride, in spite of his comments to his relative. And he supposed Miss Lister was as good a candidate as any other. Perhaps he should go ahead and propose. Get it over with. It would please his parents as well as his grandmother. So why try to hold out against the inevitable?

A vision of crystal-blue eyes came to him, and Luke could almost hear the last few chords of the song from the evening before. His heart quickened. Perhaps he should hesitate. Perhaps he should visit Brother Pierce and meet his family before he made an irrevocable decision. After his first failed attempt, it behooved him to be especially careful in selecting the girl to become his wife.

With his mind made up, Luke went to his room to gather his cloak and gloves. He would take Grandma to visit with the Listers, and then he would insist on dropping by to visit the Pierce family. Meeting the girl he'd only seen from a distance would certainly quiet the clamor in his heart.

four

Soldiers marched toward them to the *rat-a-tat* of a drumbeat. Caroline tried not to flinch at the mixture of fear and determination she saw in the faces of the men and boys. She wanted to put her arms around all of them. She wanted to gather them up and send them home to their families. They had no business here. If only she could change things. Her shoulders lifted and fell in a heartfelt sigh.

"We'd better get out of the way." Ma nodded toward the mercantile. "Let's see if we can find some sugar. The cook says she has a few sweet potatoes left from the last harvest, and she wants to make a pie."

"I love sweet potato pie." Tory's skirts swayed as she crossed the street in front of them.

"It would be a treat." Caroline took her mother's arm. "But it is getting harder and harder to find supplies."

Ma glanced back at the soldiers. "When most of the menfolk are marching to war instead of planting and harvesting crops, shortages are to be expected."

Tory held the door open until all three of them were inside. "Maybe we'll be lucky today."

"What can I help you ladies with?" A gray-haired man with a round stomach approached them.

Caroline looked around the large room lined with shelves. Empty shelves. It didn't look to her as though he had anything to sell.

The merchant's gaze followed hers around the store. "Yes, things are a bit scarce, but we're doing the best we can. Now that the winter is about to end, maybe we'll be able to get some fresh produce."

"We'll pray so." Her mother stepped forward. "We are on a mission for a five-pound bag of sugar."

The merchant bowed. "Right this way." He turned and led them toward the counter. "I just received a supply last week. But I have to admit it is a bit dear. Hard to get things brought in when the railroads are closed."

Caroline gasped. "The trains are not running?"

Tory's mouth dropped open, and she turned to her mother. "How will we get home next week?"

"I knew we should not have come." Caroline slapped a hand over her mouth, but it was too late. The words had already slipped out.

Ma bent a frown on both of them. "Don't worry. We will manage."

"I didn't mean to frighten you ladies." The man twisted his apron in his hands. "Where are you from?"

"We live in Jackson."

He looked over their heads.

Caroline wanted to turn around to see what he was looking at, but she refrained.

After a moment he refocused on them and smiled. "I was trying to remember what I'd heard about the Vicksburg to Jackson line. I think it's still running, although there may not be many seats left open for civilians."

Tory sniffed. "I don't want to be stuck in Vicksburg."

Ma shot a look at Caroline before turning to the merchant. "We'll need that sugar now, sir. How much is it?"

While Ma bartered with him, Caroline put her arm around Tory. "It's going to be okay. You know God is watching over us. No matter whether we're here or in Jackson, or even back in Natchez, the important thing is that we're together."

"I suppose so." Tory looked up at her, tears swimming in her eyes. "I just want the war to end, Caroline."

"So do I." She hugged her little sister tightly and led her back to the front door. "Let's go outside and watch the soldiers marching. They'll love seeing a pretty girl wave to them."

She was rewarded with a giggle. "Two pretty girls."

The sun was beginning to sink toward the western horizon, and a cold breeze whipped down the street as they waved at the boys in gray. The sidewalk was more crowded now than it had been earlier as the townspeople came out to cheer for the soldiers. Instead of staying on the wooden sidewalk to watch, the sisters stepped onto the street where they could see better.

It almost felt like a Fourth of July celebration with the prancing horses and marching men. Except that it wouldn't be so cold in July. Caroline's lips were beginning to grow numb, and she turned to look back over her shoulder to see if Ma had come out yet.

A loud noise brought her back around to gaze at the street. "What was that? It sounded like gunfire."

Tory shook her head.

A scream sounded from farther down the street, and the soldiers parted as a carriage careened around the corner. To Caroline it seemed the equipage was traveling in slow motion. She saw the eyes of the four horses as they raced to some unknown destination, saw the reins dangling between them, realized that no one sat in the driver's seat. All of this detail she took in instantly. Her heart pounded as she watched the carriage get closer to their side of the road.

She grabbed Tory's shoulders and pushed hard to get her safely back on the sidewalk, but somehow her feet got tangled up in her skirt. Instead of jumping to safety alongside her sister, Caroline lost her footing. She could feel herself falling, careening out of control much like the carriage bearing down on her. The whole world seemed to shake with the pounding of the hooves. She was going to die, and she could do nothing to save herself.

In the last possible instant, something grabbed her. She slammed against something—someone—hard. The thump of a racing heart reverberated in her head. It was so close she felt it rather than heard it. An iron band across her waist stole her ability to breathe, and the flashing glimpse of worried faces whirled like the kaleidoscope her parents had given to her last Christmas.

In the midst of the chaos and danger, Caroline felt safe, treasured—the way she felt in her father's hug. A scent tickled her nose, a mixture of soap and starch—a scent that presaged spring, fresh linens, and new leaves.

Then the iron band slackened its hold, and her feet touched the wooden planks of the sidewalk. Caroline leaned back a little to see the face of her rescuer. Her breath caught. "It's you."

He frowned at her, a concerned look in his obsidian eyes. "Are you hurt?"

"I—No. . .I don't think so."

His face was barely inches away. Except for the men in her family, his face was closer than any man's face had ever been. If he moved even a tiny bit closer, his mustache would brush her cheek.

The thought stole her breath. Caroline thought she might faint from the realization. Bright flashes appeared at the corner of her vision.

"Caroline!" Tory's voice penetrated her awareness. She felt something pulling on her arm. "Unhand my sister!"

The arm slipped away from her instantly. An impulse to throw herself at the handsome stranger washed through her, but her sister's grip on her arm was like an anchor keeping her from straying into dangerous waters.

"I'm sorry, miss." He bowed to Tory. "I meant no harm."

With every second that passed, she was regaining her senses. Caroline shook off her sister's hand. "You saved me from certain death."

He turned back to her and bowed once more, his charming smile lifting the edges of his lips. "I'm glad to have been of service, ma'am."

The door of the mercantile flew open, and her mother descended on them like an angry hornet. "What's going on out here? Caroline? Tory? Are you all right?"

"Yes, Mother." Caroline could not tear her gaze from the stranger's face. A part of her wanted to touch his side-whiskers, trace a finger along the edges of his mouth. Blood rushed to her cheeks. What had come over her? She blinked to break the connection between them.

"Caroline was nearly run down by a driverless carriage." Tory's voice shook with fear. "She shoved me out of the way, but she fell. I thought she was about to die."

"Thanks to the fast actions of this kind man, everything has turned out fine." The words were coming from her mouth, but she had no idea how.

Ma moved closer as though to insert herself between Caroline and the stranger. "It seems I owe you much, sir. I am Abigail Pierce." She held out her hand.

The stranger bowed over it, showing that he was well versed in social graces. "Luke Talbot, at your service, Mrs. Pierce. It's a pleasure to meet you and your lovely daughters."

The wary look on Ma's face faded. She allowed a smile to turn up the corners of her mouth. "The pleasure belongs to me, sir, especially since you saved Caroline from a nasty accident."

Although Ma was standing between them, Caroline could still see his eyes. Their gazes met, and her breath stopped again. She put a hand to her throat.

"I hope you'll allow me to escort you ladies to your home. It would be remiss of me to leave you standing here when it is obvious Miss Pierce is not completely recovered."

Caroline turned her gaze on her mother, her chest filling with hope.

"I suppose that would be acceptable, Mr. Talbot—"

"Captain Talbot, ma'am."

"You're a soldier?" Tory's voice now held more than a hint of hero worship.

He smiled and nodded. "Although I'm on furlough right now, I am pleased to serve the Confederate army."

"I know Mr. Pierce will want to add his thanks to my own, Captain." Ma's voice was firm. Caroline recognized the tone. Captain Pierce would be going back to the hotel with them unless he had a very compelling excuse.

"I'd be delighted to make his acquaintance."

"Excellent." Ma pulled on her gloves. "As soon as the supplies are loaded, we can leave."

Captain Talbot walked out onto the street and said a few words to the soldiers who were still milling about. He pointed an arm, and a couple of them went running in the direction of the driverless carriage. The others shouldered their weapons and marched east toward the outskirts of town.

Caroline was impressed with his capable handling of the situation. From the time he'd arrived on the scene, Captain Talbot had commanded the respect and admiration of all those around him. He was obviously a leader. . .and obviously well above the type of man she could hope to have for a husband.

Her sigh brought Tory a step closer. "Are you certain you're unhurt? I could not even scream when I saw that runaway carriage hurtling toward you." She took Caroline's hand in her own. "You sacrificed your own safety for me."

"You would have done the same." Caroline shifted slightly. She didn't deserve any praise. She'd only done what came naturally. The one who deserved the praise was the captain. She was not his kin, but he'd risked everything for her safety.

She glanced toward him once again as he strode back over to them and engaged their mother in easy conversation. She would enjoy whatever time and attention he gave her and her family, no matter that the outcome would probably leave her pining for more. Like the woman who petitioned Jesus for help, she would gladly accept the crumbs Captain Talbot let fall while he was near.

five

"I can hardly believe the week is nearing an end." Grandma sat in the rocker and pushed at the floor with her foot. "Where has the time gone?"

Luke opened his eyes wide. "We've been inundated with visits from your friends every morning. And shortly after lunch, we have made calls on anyone in town who has a marriageable daughter. Then it's back to the hotel for a quick supper before we go to the church to hear the pastor. I am exhausted by the time I climb into my bed, and it seems my head hardly rests on the pillow before the sun is up and it's time to start all over again."

"If there's one thing I have learned in my life, it is—to quote one of John Heywood's proverbs—'Take time whan time cometh, lest time steale away.'"

"Good advice." Luke walked to the window and stared out at the street below. The townspeople were making for their homes as the sun set on the far side of the river. The activity looked normal, ordinary, as though the war was over. But he knew better. "My furlough will be over by the end of the month."

"All the more reason to find a suitable wife now." The rocker creaked rhythmically behind him. "No one will travel out to Shady Oaks to visit us. The risk of being caught by a Yankee patrol increases daily."

"Perhaps we should cut our visit short." Luke turned away from the window. "I want to make certain the plantation is in good shape before I have to leave you alone."

Grandma waved a dismissive hand. "I was alone before you got here, young man. I can make it on my own if I have to. Besides, if you will settle on one of the young ladies you've met, I won't have to be alone. Your new wife and I will work in tandem to make sure you have a home to return to."

Luke considered her carefully. "I'm not sure you're willing to give over the reins to some young miss."

"You're wrong about that. There's plenty of work to go around. When I married your grandfather and he brought me down to Mississippi, I had no idea how to run a household. His mother was not very welcoming, and I had a hard few years until your mother was born. Even though all of that happened many decades ago, I still remember what it was like. I am especially well qualified to help your wife find her feet."

"That's a relief." He walked to the rocker and bent to place a kiss on his grandmother's cheek. "But what if I choose someone you don't approve of?"

"I cannot imagine your being so foolish. Your parents raised you to be levelheaded and to know your duty." She patted his cheek. "You'll make an excellent choice."

Luke straightened and pulled out his pocket watch. "I suppose it's time for me to change into my dress clothes if we're to make it to the Lancasters' home before midnight."

"Why don't you wear your uniform tonight?"

A frown creased his brow. "I don't think that's proper as long as I'm on furlough."

"Fiddle!" Grandma pushed herself up. "You are an officer of the Confederacy. Are you ashamed to show your true colors?"

Luke straightened his shoulders. "Not at all, I jus—"

"I don't want to hear any excuses," she interrupted him. "The ladies will love it. And I have a yen to see you in it myself."

Swallowing his arguments, Luke bowed to her. "I will do as you wish, Grandmother." He could see how much she wanted him to wear his uniform. He would have to get past his discomfort and put a good face on the matter. It wouldn't do to let any of the townspeople sense discord between them.

❧

The uniform was a bit snugger than it had been the last time he wore it. Luke tugged on the short jacket as he entered the ballroom. He had been far too lazy over the past months. It was time to get back to Shady Oaks and get the plantation in order. He could find a suitable wife when the war was over. Grandma might be anxious to have someone with her during these troubling times, but he didn't think he'd be stationed that far away.

The room was already full. The musicians played in one corner while the older men stood in tight groups in the opposite corner. In between, couples danced under the watchful gazes of their chaperones. Looking at the people here, one would hardly believe a devastating war was taking the lives of their husbands and sons.

The music came to a rousing end, and he spotted Miss Lister being led from the dance floor. Her escort was a slender man with a wide mustache and wavy black hair. Luke frowned as he watched Miss Lister smile up at him.

"Are you jealous she's caught the attention of Major Fontenot?" A hand clapped him on the back.

"Hamp, what are you doing here?" Luke shook hands with the man who'd traveled south at the same time he had come to take over his grandparents' plantation. They'd found out during the long train ride that they were bound for the same area and had become fast friends. Hampton Boothe had a head of carroty-hued hair that curled in spite of the copious amounts of Macassar oil he applied. It was the bane of his existence.

"Thought I'd come see what you might be up to." Hamp grinned at him. "Looks like the rumors are true."

"What rumors?"

"That you've fallen head over heels for the lovely Miss Lister."

Luke punched him on the shoulder. "And what if I have?"

Grabbing his shoulder in mock pain, Hamp made a face. "Nothing, nothing at all. Far be it from me to try and stop a man from hanging a noose around his own neck."

"Matrimony is not a noose. It's a state of endless joy."

Hamp snorted.

"Check the poets if you don't believe me."

"Matrimony could be nice, I suppose, but I don't know that you should be tying yourself to Marianna Lister for life."

All humor left Luke in a rush. "Do you know something detrimental about the lady?"

"Only that her beautiful face may hide a waspish nature."

Luke rolled his eyes. "Do you think I would be ruled by my wife?"

A shrug answered him. "I'm not saying that. But you might want to choose someone a bit more biddable."

"If I cannot rule my household, I deserve to be hen-pecked." Luke turned away with the intention of finding Miss Lister and asking her for a dance, but a commotion at the entrance to the ballroom stopped him.

Everyone was crowding around the tall couple at the door. Wondering what was happening, he took a few steps in that direction before he recognized them. It was Brother Pierce and his wife. Mrs. Pierce caught his gaze and smiled at him before turning to say something to the young lady who had come up on her other side.

Caroline Pierce. His heart skipped a beat. She was a vision of loveliness this evening. He'd thought she was pretty when he saw her at the church, but tonight she was stunning.

"Who is that?" Hamp's voice behind him was full of curiosity and wonder. "I've never seen her before."

"You ought to spend more time in church." Luke threw his answer over his shoulder as he made his way to where she stood.

Miss Pierce looked as scared as she had when he pulled her from the path of the runaway carriage earlier this week. Everything in him wanted to rescue her once again. He bowed to Mrs. Pierce. "May I have the honor of dancing with your daughter?"

"I. . .I don—"

"It's a pleasure to see you again, Captain Talbot." Mrs. Pierce turned to her daughter. "You cannot break a soldier's heart, dearest. You must give him a sweet memory to take with him when he returns to the battlefield."

Although her cheeks had reddened at the gentle scold, Caroline Pierce nodded and held out her hand.

Luke tucked it into the crook of his arm and led her to the edge of the dance floor. "I count myself lucky to secure the first dance with you. I'm sure you will be flooded with offers when I return you to your parents' side."

Her gaze darted upward to meet his. "Are you making fun of me?"

"Not at all." Luke was stunned. Did she have no idea how beautiful she looked? The dark blue of her dress made her eyes glow like sapphires. Her golden hair seemed to radiate under the light of the candles. He wanted to tell her how beautiful she was, but he had the feeling his compliments might frighten her even more.

The orchestra began a waltz, and Luke swept her into his embrace. She fit in his arms as though made for him. He started off slowly to make certain she could keep up with him. She seemed so innocent he would not have been shocked to learn this was her first ball. But if so, she had been well schooled in the art of waltzing. He twirled her faster and faster, but her steps never faltered. It was as though she knew before he did which way he was going to move.

"You are an excellent dancer, Miss Pierce."

"Thank you, Captain Talbot."

A few more measures followed in silence. All he could see of his dance partner was the top of her head and her wide skirts. Her face was hidden from his view as she apparently found his buttons fascinating.

"I find myself very comfortable with you, Miss Pierce. Most of the other young ladies I have danced with seem to feel it is necessary to chatter endlessly about the most obscure things. You, however, are to be commended for your reticence. It is a charming characteristic."

She did not glance up.

He swung her around again. "Is there something wrong with my jacket?"

Caroline shook her head. "Not at all."

He squeezed her hand briefly. "That's a relief. My grandmother asked me to wear this uniform. She felt I was not handsome enough unless I wore something a bit more dashing than evening wear."

She glanced up then, her eyes wide. "But you are the most handsome man here."

"Thank you, Miss Pierce." He smiled at the words. Her tone of voice was matter-of-fact without the slightest hint of flattery. A warm feeling flooded him. Luke wanted to laugh out loud. He wanted to hold Miss Pierce close to his heart. He wanted to get lost in her blue gaze. The thoughts filling his head both intrigued and scared him.

But what did he know about this girl? She could sing. Her

father was a well-known pastor. She was willing to sacrifice her safety for the sake of a family member. Those were all points in her favor, but they didn't guarantee she would make a good wife. He needed to know more. "Where did you grow up, Miss Pierce?"

"In Jackson, but I was born in Natchez."

"I see." He looked up to see his grandmother frowning at him. Odd that she was not happy. He was doing what she wanted—talking to a marriageable young lady. "I haven't been to Natchez. Is it the same as Vicksburg?"

Miss Pierce hesitated a moment before shaking her head. "Natchez feels more. . .more staid. Or maybe I feel that way because I know Natchez was settled so long ago."

He chuckled. "Vicksburg has been around for a while, too."

"Yes, that's true. But the homes here have a newer feeling to them. The riverfront is much the same at both towns—high bluffs overlooking the river."

"Do you still have family in Natchez?"

She nodded. "My brother and his family live at Magnolia. He runs the plantation now that my grandparents have gotten older."

Miss Pierce seemed tailor-made for him. She was quiet and biddable, and her family sounded much like his own.

The music came to a close before he could think of other questions, but Luke was impressed with what he'd learned. He took her back to her mother and stood there a moment, talking to both ladies.

"Why, if it isn't the dashing Captain Talbot."

Luke turned to find Miss Lister bearing down on him, her skirts swaying as she managed to plant herself between him and Miss Pierce. It was not the smartest move. Marianna's cream dress was probably more fashionable than the one worn by Miss Pierce, but he had to avert his eyes from the charms she was exhibiting above the low neckline. Instead of being alluring, it made her look a bit tawdry and desperate.

"Good evening, Miss Lister. Have you met Mrs. Pierce and Miss Pierce?"

She raised her chin and attempted to stare down her nose at the two ladies. "I do not believe—Oh, yes, you're the preacher's wife, aren't you?"

"Indeed." Mrs. Pierce's eyes flashed. She drew herself up and looked past Miss Lister. "And I believe I hear my husband calling to us now. Please excuse us."

Her smile seemed a bit forced, but Luke could not blame Mrs. Pierce. He wished he could follow her and Miss Pierce across the room, but Miss Lister had her hand on his arm. He felt a little like a hooked fish as he watched the two women make their way to the far side of the ballroom.

"I have something to confess, Captain Talbot." Miss Lister's voice was as sweet as cane syrup.

Luke brought his attention back to the girl next to him, careful to keep his gaze trained on her face. "I am almost afraid to ask what you wish to tell me."

She snapped open a fan with her free hand and used it to hide the bottom half of her face. "I have been counting the minutes until I could see you once more."

It was only with an effort that he kept his mouth from dropping open. What kind of change had come over Miss Lister? Where was the charming companion who he had thought might become Mrs. Talbot? She had always been a little forward, but he'd never thought her so brash.

He remembered Hamp's warning. What was he to do now? He could not be rude to her.

"You are very kind, Miss Lister."

The musicians had taken a break, but now they began playing once more.

He sketched a bow. "Will you honor me with a dance?"

She giggled behind her fan and nodded.

As he led her to the center of the room, he thought it was lucky this was not a waltz. He took his position to her left as prescribed by the polonaise and held her right hand. Then it was bow-step-step, bow-step-step, bow-step-step-change in the slow movements of the dance. Miss Lister smiled and even tried to move a bit closer a couple of times, but Luke always managed to keep the proper distance between them. He didn't know when he'd ever found a dance so interminable. As soon as it ended, he escorted Miss Lister back to her mother and left her side as quickly as possible.

He managed to partner several other young ladies, although he remembered neither their names nor the conversations. But when he saw his redheaded friend chatting with Miss Pierce, he stumbled and had to apologize to his unfortunate partner. When the musicians took yet another break, he looked around for Miss Pierce in her stunning blue dress but could find her nowhere. His heart wilted. He'd wanted more time with her and had planned to ask her to join him at the midnight repast. Had her parents already taken her home?

He sauntered over to the corner where the widows sat together, their fans waving like butterflies in a field of flowers. He sat in a vacant chair next to his grandmother, thinking to escort her to the dining room since Miss Pierce was not available. "Are you having a good time tonight?"

She pierced him with a frown. "Why have you not been paying more attention to Marianna? I thought you had fixed your interest with her."

Her reproachful tone and pointed complaint made blood surge upward, heating his cheeks and his ears. "Many young ladies of good families are in attendance this evening. Did you expect me to ignore them?"

"Of course not, but you have only danced with Miss Lister once. After all the time you have spent with her, you've raised certain hopes. I would hate to see you disappoint her family or yours by letting your head be turned by some pretentious upstart."

Anger started a slow burn in his belly. Even though they were surrounded by people, or maybe because of that fact, Luke decided it was time to take a stand with her. "I do not care for your tone of voice, Grandmother. You seem to have the mistaken belief you can choose my dance partners. You have no say in the matter at all."

He saw the shock in her expression, but he would not back down from his statements. He realized his desire to give his grandmother respect had evolved into a situation where she felt she was in control of him. It was about time to set her straight on that matter. He was a grown man, and she would respect his position of authority.

Grandma's fan fluttered back and forth with some force as she digested his words.

He noticed the ladies sitting nearby had stopped talking to each other and were avidly awaiting her response.

She opened her mouth once and then closed it before swallowing hard. "You are quite right, Luke. I didn't mean to overstate my concern. It's only that I love you so much. You are my only grandson, and the continuation of our family rests solely on your capable shoulders. Please forgive me."

The other ladies went back to the conversation almost as soon as they realized he and Grandma were not going to have a row.

Luke nodded and leaned over to plant a kiss her cheek. "I love you, too. I was about to go get something to eat. Would you care to join me?"

She nodded, so he stood and helped her to her feet. As

they approached the dining room, he listened with one ear to her chatter about the number of people in attendance and their social standing in the community.

Luke hoped his earlier words had not hurt her too much, and although he regretted airing the matter in such a public setting, she should not have chastised him so openly. His pride would not allow him to appear too weak to control his own family members.

&

Caroline knew the moment Captain Talbot entered the dining room. The room seemed to contract until the only thing she could see was his dark hair and dashing gray uniform. Her heart pounded in her chest as she saw him smile down at his companion. His grandmother, she had learned. Wasn't that sweet? And another indication of what a good man he was.

She wished no one was sitting next to her, but her parents were seated on one side of her and Hampton Boothe, a young man she'd just met this evening, had claimed the seat to her left. He seemed a kind and outgoing sort, the type of companion her younger sister would adore. Mr. Boothe was well read, and his lively sense of humor had made her smile several times.

"My friend has been telling me how wonderful your father's sermons are." Mr. Boothe's voice recaptured her attention.

"I believe so." She dipped her spoon into her bowl of oyster stew. "Of course, I may not be an impartial judge of the matter. Pa says he started preaching for the wrong reason, but God had the right reason in mind all along."

"What is the right reason?"

Caroline looked at his earnest face. "Are you a Christian, Mr. Boothe?"

"I suppose so. When I was a boy, one of those traveling

preachers came through here and stayed with me and my family. Before he left, he took all of us out back to a creek and baptized us. All I remember was him raising his hand and asking me if I wanted to be forgiven so I could go to heaven. I knew the right answer was yes so that's what I said. Then he prayed to God and dunked me in that water. When he pulled me back up, he said I was a new person."

"Did he ask you if you believed in Christ as the one and only Son of God and the way to salvation?"

Mr. Boothe frowned for a moment before shaking his head. "I don't remember that part. Is it important? Do I need to get baptized again?"

Lord, please give me the right words. "Getting baptized is important, and I know some folks who've done it more than once, but it's not necessary for salvation. It's your belief that makes the difference. The day Jesus was crucified, He wasn't the only one being put to death. Two criminals hung on crosses beside him at Golgotha. One of them scorned Jesus, but the other one recognized Him and asked for forgiveness. Even though he had not been baptized, Jesus told the second man: 'Today shalt thou be with me in paradise.'"

"So it's okay to wait until you're dying to decide whether or not you believe in Jesus."

Caroline forgot all about the food in front of her. She forgot about Captain Talbot. She even forgot to be self-conscious. "Of course not. That would be utter foolishness. First of all, you would miss so many opportunities to live right and so many blessings that the Lord wants to give you. And then what if you die suddenly, before you get the chance to turn to Christ? Do you want to take the risk and end up spending eternity separated from your Maker?"

"Sounds to me like Mr. Pierce is not the only preacher in the family."

Caroline looked over her shoulder to see Captain Talbot standing directly behind Mr. Boothe. Her breath caught. When had he come over? And why hadn't she kept her mouth shut? Now he would think she was too talkative. He'd mentioned how much he prized a female who did not chatter all the time.

Sharing the Gospel is not idle chatter. Her heart settled into a more sedate rhythm at the thought. She felt the warmth of His presence. No matter what it made Captain Talbot think, she would not feel bad for speaking out.

Her dinner companion rolled his eyes. "You're not welcome over here, Luke. Miss Pierce and I are getting along fine without your interruption. I doubt you have anything to add, and I need to hear what she's got to say about faith. We live in uncertain times, and you never know when you might be drawing your last breath."

"What foolishness is this?" Captain Talbot raised one eyebrow. "I'll admit I haven't known you long, Boothe, but this is an obvious ploy to impress Miss Pierce." He turned his warm gaze to her. "He's got a reputation as a freethinker, you know."

Mr. Boothe's mouth dropped open. "I am no such thing."

"Is that so?" Captain Talbot shook his head. "Then why don't you tell us how many of her father's church meetings you have attended this week, Hampton."

"What?" Mr. Boothe spluttered. "I...well...I..."

Caroline felt a little sorry for the man sitting next to her. He was obviously flustered by the question. She was about to answer for him, but the captain forestalled her with a wink.

"See what I mean, Miss Pierce?" His voice was full of triumph. "Don't let him fool you."

Was the handsome captain flirting with her? Caroline thought he might be. A pleasant glow brought a smile to her face. She gave an exaggerated sigh. "I suppose you will have to come to the revival meeting tomorrow afternoon, Mr. Boothe, to prove your sincerity."

Now it was Mr. Boothe who looked pleased. He shot a triumphant glance toward Captain Talbot. "I would love to attend."

Caroline decided to take the middle road. She did not want the serious matter of salvation to be diluted by foolishness. "My family would be happy to see both of you there."

"Might I hope you will also be glad to see me there?" Mr. Boothe touched her hand where it lay on the table between them.

Certain her cheeks were as red as a bowl of strawberries, Caroline pulled her hand away and tucked it in her lap. "How could I not be? All Christians rejoice over the salvation of a lost soul."

"Save me a place up front, if you will, Miss Pierce." Captain Talbot smiled. "I can hardly wait to see how Hampton reacts to Brother Pierce's sermon."

As he walked off, her mother leaned toward Caroline. "What a fine young man that Captain Talbot is, and he seems quite smitten with you, dearest."

Caroline glanced toward Mr. Boothe, glad to see he was chatting with the person on his far side. She put her hands to her cheeks in an attempt to cool them. "You misunderstand, Ma. We were discussing faith and Pa's sermons."

"I'm neither blind nor so old that I cannot see when someone, or even a pair of someones, is interested in my daughter."

Wondering if she could disappear under the table, Caroline shook her head but remained silent. She was certain her mother was mistaken. Neither man had been more than polite.

Yet there had been a special gleam in the captain's obsidian eyes. A gleam that made her breath catch.

What if? A tiny smile teased the edges of her mouth. The very idea that either the sweet Mr. Boothe or the debonair Captain Talbot might be interested in her was at the same time terrifying and exhilarating.

six

Luke smiled across the table toward Caroline. "I'm glad your parents agreed to let you and your sister attend lunch with my grandmother and me."

"Me, too."

Her blush was endearing. It hinted at her innocence, a refreshing change from the calculated charm he usually encountered from the local belles. Caroline Pierce was different from all of them. Different from any young woman he'd ever met. He admired her quiet competence and the faith shining in her blue eyes.

Was this why he'd been unable to quash his ardent pursuit? It had been only two days since he'd seen her at the Lancasters' ball, but already he had paid a visit to her parents and invited her to today's luncheon.

"Have you seen many battles, Captain Talbot?"

The eager question posed by her younger sister turned his attention to Tory. He nodded. "Far too many."

"It's a shame the Yankees won't just let us alone." Grandma heaped a steaming spoonful of collard greens on top of her cornbread before handing the bowl to Caroline. "Too many men have died already."

A frown crossed Tory's face. "I'll bet those Yankees run whenever they see our handsome soldiers riding toward them on the battlefield."

Luke considered his answer. He didn't want to disillusion the younger Miss Pierce, but there was nothing romantic about war. "It's not like that, Miss Tory. The Union soldiers

55

are as brave as any of our men. We all follow the orders of our commanding officers even if it means death."

He noticed Caroline's shudder and wished he could reach across the square table and squeeze her hand. He wanted to comfort her, but since his grandmother was present, he contented himself with a wide smile.

"Let's talk about something more pleasant, shall we?" Luke accepted the bowl of collards from Tory, but his gaze remained focused on Caroline. "Tell us about growing up in Jackson. Have you ever visited the capitol?"

"Yes, many times. Ma and Pa are very interested in keeping abreast of the political situation." Her answering smile was like sunshine after a week of rain. "They say it's the duty of all Americans to take part in the democratic process on which this country was founded."

"Do they not consider themselves to be Confederate Americans?" Grandma's voice was sharp with disapproval.

Caroline's cheeks reddened. "I suppose so. But they don't approve of slavery."

Luke was surprised at the admission. Abolitionists were not unheard of in Mississippi, but they were few in number. Too many people here relied on slave labor to make their farms and plantations successful.

"I had heard as much." Grandma's right hand played with her fork. "And that your grandparents in Natchez hold even more radical ideas than your parents."

"I suppose you could say that." Caroline seemed so engrossed with the food on her plate that she could not tear her gaze away from it. "Our grandfather freed all of the slaves on his plantation a long time ago and offered them paying jobs."

Luke's mouth dropped open. "I doubt that made him very popular."

"Oh no." Caroline looked at him, her eyes wide. "In fact, the townspeople once tried to burn our grandfather out. Our grandmother risked her reputation and her very life to warn him."

Tory picked up the story. "They stopped the fire. It was a very brave thing to do. If not for her, Magnolia would have burned to the ground with our grandfather inside the main house." In her excitement, Tory made a wide gesture with her hands. Her right hand bumped her glass of lemonade and it teetered. "Oh!"

Luke tried to prevent disaster, but her flailing hand prevented him from reaching the overturning glass.

From the corner of his eye, he saw Caroline cover her mouth with her hand, but then his focus centered on the unfolding disaster as Tory jumped up, her jerky actions further disturbing their table. The surface tilted toward his grandmother, all of its contents sliding inexorably toward her lap.

Grandma's loaded dinner plate was the first missile to land, followed by plates of cornbread, smoked ham, and stewed apples. The bowl of collard greens tumbled toward her, too, but Luke managed to catch the hot vegetables before they reached the edge of the table. He was not so lucky with the butter crock or the salt cellar, both of which crashed to the floor, blasting their contents across his grandmother's dress, face, and hair.

Tory was frozen, her hands covering her mouth, but her sister jumped up and began picking up the remnants of the food and crockery. "I am s—so sorry."

Grandma pulled a handkerchief from the sleeve of her dress and dabbed at the mess on her face. "It's not you who needs to apologize. It wasn't your fault. But I trust your sister will be severely punished for her shenanigans."

Luke opened his mouth to speak up for the young girl

who was now crying quietly, but he was forestalled by Caroline. At his grandmother's words, her head went up and the fire of battle entered her blue eyes. "I beg your pardon?"

"You heard me." Grandma sniffed. "In my day she would be restricted to her room with a diet of bread and water for her unspeakable actions."

Tory began crying in earnest now. Caroline turned her back on his grandmother and stalked over to her sister. "Don't worry, dear. It was only an accident." She looked at Luke. "I think we should return to our hotel."

Luke wondered what had happened to the shy preacher's daughter. He'd never expected to see such determination, such righteous indignation. She was as fierce as any soldier in the midst of battle, eager to defend the innocent.

This was a side of Caroline he'd never dreamed existed, a side he had to admire. Would she leap to the defense of anyone she cared about? He rather thought she might. Beneath her quiet exterior lurked a heart of gold—a treasure to be sought by any man who was looking for a suitable woman to marry.

❧

Caroline had never felt such anticipation before a ball. She had dreaded going to the Lancasters'. . .but tonight was different. She grabbed her fan and reticule and headed downstairs to join her parents.

Only Pa was standing in the hallway. "Your mother is already in the carriage." He took her hand and put it on his arm. "You look especially beautiful tonight, Caroline."

She dipped her head but said nothing. Fathers always thought their daughters were beautiful—at least her father did.

Being careful not to lose control of her hoops, Caroline settled into the seat opposite her mother and listened as her parents discussed returning to Jackson before the end of the month. Her heart sank. She would never see Captain Talbot again once they left Vicksburg.

Her mother turned to Caroline. "You're very quiet this evening."

Pa fingered the edge of his cravat. "She's going to be the belle of the ball."

"Not if Miss Lister is in attendance. She is much prettier than I and more accomplished by all accounts." What she didn't say was she still hoped to see Captain Talbot. After the luncheon with him and his grandmother three days prior, she had been unable to banish him from her thoughts. He was such a considerate man. And so handsome she had to remind herself not to stare at him. He was intelligent, too. It was a wonder no female had managed to win his affections. Perhaps it was the Lord's plan. Perhaps he would fall in love with her and—

Caroline halted the thought. It was silly to have such ideas. No one fell in love at first sight. Never mind the way seeing him made her heart throb. She wouldn't be able to stay in Vicksburg long enough for him to develop deep feelings for her. She sighed. Luke Talbot was certain to fall in love with someone else—someone like the beauteous Miss Lister.

The carriage came to a halt, and Caroline leaned forward to catch a glimpse of the Abbot home. It was an imposing mansion perched high on a bluff overlooking a bend in the Mississippi River. Lamps shone in every window of the two-story brick house and lined the circular driveway, lending a fairy-tale appearance to the estate. As she alighted and followed her parents up the wide stairs, Caroline felt like a princess.

The sensation persisted as she smiled at their hosts and complimented them on their home. She was pronounced a lovely young lady and sent inside to break the hearts of all the young men.

Dozens of couples were already dancing to the melodious sounds of the orchestra. Other guests stood in small groups of two or more, renewing acquaintances or discussing whatever topics were popular—the war mostly.

A couple about the same age as Ma and Pa approached them. After introductions, they launched into a discussion of the church's stance on slavery. It was a touchy subject, but one that held little interest for Caroline.

"I hope your sister has recovered from your visit three days ago."

The deep tones made Caroline's breath catch. He was here, and he'd sought her out. She turned to give him her brightest smile. "Yes, Captain. Thank you for asking. She was devastated to have caused such a mess, but youth is resilient."

"Yes, indeed." The look in his eyes brought a flutter to her stomach. "My only regret was that our visit was cut short by her accident. I would have liked to spend more time with you."

Caroline raised her fan to hide her blush. He probably thought she was a poor, dumb provincial. She wished she had more self-control. What kind of woman blushed because someone complimented her?

"Will you dance with me?"

Caroline glanced at her mother for permission and received a nod.

A waltz was playing as they joined the other dancers. Captain Talbot's arm was a warm band around her waist. He was so strong and confident. She made the mistake of meeting his glance. The admiration she saw in his eyes was almost too much to bear. Her heart was galloping faster than a racing horse. In that moment she knew the truth. Love at first sight might not exist, but she had fallen in love with Luke Talbot. The realization made her miss a step, but he held her close and kept her from stumbling. She wished the song would last forever.

When it ended, they were near a pair of doors opening out onto a balcony. "It's a bit warm in here. Would you like to step outside for a moment?"

Caroline's heart skidded to a sudden stop. Dare she go outside with him? She glanced toward her parents, who were deep in conversation. Excitement at her daring coursed through Caroline. "Only for a moment."

He swept her out of the room instantly, his hand resting lightly at the center of her back. "I hope you know the effect you've had on me over the past days." His face was so close she could feel his breath on her cheek.

Had she made a mistake in agreeing to come outside alone with him? Did he think she was brazen? Caroline moved to the balustrade. "Perhaps we should go back inside."

"Please give me a moment. I have something I'd like to say to you."

The air cooled her arms even though they were covered with elbow-length gloves. Caroline rubbed them as she watched him. "Is something wrong?"

He stepped closer and took her hands in his. Then he did something so unexpected that she could not believe her eyes. . . .

He dropped to one knee. "I can't get you out of my mind, Caroline. Since the first time I saw you, I have had eyes for no woman but you. You are beautiful, talented, and so pure. I know we've only known each other a few days, but I hope you'll believe me when I say I don't think I can live the rest of my life unless you're by my side. I wish we had more time, but life is far too uncertain these days. I cannot risk the chance that we'll be separated, so please say you'll do me the honor of becoming my wife."

Tears threatened to overwhelm her. "Luke." This was her

dream come true. This was the fairy tale. This was the man God had created for her. And he was asking her to be his wife. He loved her! It was almost too good to be true. Yet there he was, looking up at her, the love evident on his face. How could she turn him down?

"Please say yes, Caroline."

Where she had been cold a few moments earlier, now a fire burned her skin. Luke's words had changed everything. "Yes." She nodded for emphasis. "Yes, Luke. I will marry you, as soon as we get Pa's approval."

He stood up and took her in his arms. "You've made me the happiest man alive. I want to marry you right away." He pressed a kiss on her temple.

Her toes curled, and Caroline thought she might faint. She nodded again as her eyes drifted shut. She had to be dreaming, but the man holding her felt very solid. A small voice warned her that it was too fast, but she suppressed it. She was in love with a man who loved her. What could possibly go wrong?

seven

"I know a secret." Tory's words brought a frown to Caroline's face. She shook her head at her little sister.

"Then you should honor your promise to keep it." Mrs. Pierce plied her needle with measured precision, never looking up from the sock she was darning. "A promise is like an oath. God has many warnings against breaking an oath."

"But I didn't promise to keep it."

"Tory. . ." Caroline heard the plea in her own voice. She didn't want her parents to find out until Luke could be here, too. She glanced at the clock on the mantel. It seemed to have stopped its forward movement. Would the morning never end? His meeting with the major was supposed to be over before lunch. If he didn't arrive soon, it would be too late. She'd never been able to keep anything from her mother. Ma seemed able to read her mind with a single glance.

As if she had already discerned something, Ma looked up, her gaze shifting between her daughters. "Please don't tell me. . . ."

Caroline's head went up. How did she do that? She held her shoulders straight as though about to face a firing squad. Her stomach knotted. "I have nothing to tell you right now."

"Is it about that boy who rescued you? The soldier?" Ma's gaze pierced her. "Have you agreed to marry him?"

Her lips trembled. Why was this so difficult? Why couldn't she simply say the words? Where was her courage? "I. . . p–prefer to w–wait for C–Captain Talbot's arrival." Only eight words, but she was winded.

63

Ma stood up and moved to the sofa, where she sat next to her sister. "Tory, you are excused."

"But Ma—"

"You heard me. Now go. I need to talk to your sister." Ma didn't say anything else until Tory's lagging footsteps made it to the hallway and the door to the ladies' parlor was closed behind her.

She took the sampler Caroline had been working on and put it on the low table in front of the sofa. Then she gathered Caroline's hands in her own. "Tell me what happened."

Caroline took a quick breath. "I love him, Ma." Not a single stutter. Perhaps shallow breaths were the answer.

"I know you think you do, but Caroline, you don't know anything about him."

She pulled her hands free and stood. "I know he's a good man. A Christian man who loves me. He's also kind and thoughtful and brave besides being well educated." Caroline was beginning to feel a little lightheaded, so she stopped talking.

"I see you've thought about this." The ticking of the clock was louder than her mother's comment.

Caroline held her hands out to the fire. "Yes, ma'am."

Ma sighed. "Your pa would say I brought this on myself by begging you to stand up for yourself."

From where she stood, Caroline could see through the window overlooking the entrance to their hotel. She watched a carriage pull up, hoping she would see Luke's handsome face, but the lady who got out was a stranger.

She felt rather than heard her mother get up and walk toward her. An arm went around her waist, and her mother pulled her close. "And I guess he would be right."

Their shared laughter eased the tension.

"I love you, Caroline, and I only want the best for you."

"Luke is the best. I never thought I'd find anyone as good as Pa, but he is."

"Time will tell. As soon as we talk to your father, I'll write to your grandparents and ask them if we can have the wedding at Magnolia."

Caroline's mouth fell open. "But—"

"I know!" Her mother clapped her hands together, excitement showing on her face. "We'll have the wedding at Christmas. It's my favorite time of the year. And the plantation looks so nice when it's bedecked in garland and mistletoe."

She should have known it wouldn't be easy. She looked at her mother and considered how to break the bad news to her. "We don't want to wait, Ma."

That stopped her mother in midplan. Her eyes opened wide. "When were you thinking about marrying him?"

"Saturday." The syllables fell into a deep silence. The expressions that crossed her mother's face might have been humorous under other circumstances, but Caroline could not manage to summon up a smile. "We want Pa to perform the ceremony."

"But why the unseemly haste?"

"Luke has to return to duty in two weeks."

"I see." Her mother walked back to the sofa and sat down. "I don't suppose you could wait until after the war?"

Caroline shook her head. "Don't you remember telling me how you knew immediately Pa was right for you? Luke is the right man for me. I've prayed about it, and so has he, and we believe God has given us His blessing."

"Did you ask Him about the timing?" Ma waved her hand before Caroline could form an answer. "I'm sorry. That was uncalled for." She sighed again. "But I'm not sure the two of you are interpreting God correctly, and I'm worried you may be making the worst mistake of your life."

Caroline moved toward the sofa, confidence surging from some deep place inside her, carrying her to unprecedented heights of self-confidence. "Stop worrying, Ma. I know we're doing the right thing."

❧

" 'Wherefore they are no more twain, but one flesh.'" Rev. Pierce recited the words slowly as though testing each one. " 'What therefore God hath joined together, let not man put asunder.' "

The words reverberated in the nearly empty church with authority. There simply had not been time to have a large, lavish wedding. And with the war drawing nearer to the city, those who could afford to were leaving for what they hoped would be safer havens. Even Hampton had not been able to attend, although he had assured both Luke and Caroline that he was not jealous. And then he'd gone to great length to describe the latest lady to catch his attention.

Luke swallowed hard as Caroline's father closed his worn copy of the Bible and looked down on them with a gentle smile. *How has all this come to pass in such a short period of time?* His heart raced a little faster at the thought. He took a deep breath and turned to his bride, lifting her veil with careful movements. This was his first act as a married man, and it signified that the woman in front of him was now his responsibility.

For a moment it felt as though he looked into a stranger's face, but this was Caroline Talbot, née Pierce, the new mistress of Shady Oaks Plantation and the woman who would help him fulfill his responsibility to his family. Where was the calm serenity that had initially drawn him to Caroline? She looked like a frightened child, one who had lost her parent. Her chin quivered slightly, betraying her fear.

He squeezed one of her cold hands reassuringly, rewarded by a wan smile that he returned. He could almost feel the tension draining away from her shoulders, and his ability to ease her fears somehow made him feel more confident in his choice.

"Let us pray." Brother Pierce's voice interrupted his thoughts.

Luke bowed his head but did not close his eyes. He had been very attentive to Caroline and her family's beliefs while courting her. But the time for pretense was over. Religious beliefs were reserved for women and children and of course ministers. Luke was well aware of the fact that real men had to make their own way in this world.

He was surprised to catch the warning frown and shake of the reverend's head as the older man cleared his throat before beginning to pray. At first Luke thought the frown had been aimed at him for his lack of piety, but a rustle behind him betrayed the real target to be the irrepressible Tory. Her duties as chaperone for her older sister were now over, but he had the feeling she would continue to be a distraction for all those around her. Another reason he, his bride, and his grandmother should depart as soon as possible.

He would bet Tory was nearly dancing in the aisle behind them with poorly repressed glee at the marriage of her elder sister. And why wouldn't she be excited? Caroline had snagged one of the most eligible bachelors in Warren County, maybe in the whole state. His head dropped a bit closer to his chest at the immodest thought. *But it's true. Even with the privations of this war, Grandma and I are very comfortable. I can afford to provide anything Caroline could possibly need. I only hope things remain the same.*

". . .and may they serve as a source of love and strength to each other and the focal point of a Christian household. Amen."

Luke looked up and, at a nod from the preacher, turned to his wife. He bent and dropped a kiss on her right cheek before turning with her to face the few people seated behind them—his grandmother and the other two ladies of the Pierce household. Grandma was crying again. She had hardly stopped since he announced his intention to marry Caroline. He noticed Caroline's mother was also dabbing at her eyes with a handkerchief, but her tears seemed joyful rather than cheerless.

He wished he could believe Grandma would soon recover and put a happier face on the situation for his sake and for the sake of his new bride. After all, Grandma was the one who had pushed him to find a wife. She would have to find a way to live with the woman he'd chosen. . .whether it was the one she wanted or not. And that was the real crux of the problem. Grandma had wanted Marianna for a granddaughter-in-law. In her estimation Marianna Lister, the granddaughter of her personal crony, would make a better wife and mother than the girl standing next to him.

He believed he'd made the better choice. Marianna might seem a little more poised, but she was also more spiteful and forward than Caroline. No, it was Caroline's quiet manner and serenity that had drawn him almost from the first time he'd seen her. Luke knew what he was doing. Caroline had the morals and character to make a perfect wife and mother.

Luke pushed back a lock of his hair that had fallen across his forehead before placing his hand over the small one trembling on his arm. "My heart and devotion are yours, dear wife."

She offered a shaky smile at the reminder of her new status. "I can hardly believe it."

He had to lower his head to hear her words, and he could not resist kissing her cheek once again. A hint of lilac tickled his senses, and he breathed it in. Like so much else about his new bride, the scent was understated and subtle, only appreciated by those closest to her. She was so different from the other girls he'd met.

A brief pang struck at him as he thought of the girl in Tennessee, but he pushed it aside. He'd made his choice. Amelia was his past, Caroline his future.

His grandmother stopped crying long enough to snap open her fan and ply it with sufficient force to raise a small breeze. "Now that it's done, shall we go back to the hotel for the wedding breakfast? Luke, you know we'll need to get on the road soon if we are to arrive at Shady Oaks before nightfall." She shuddered. "I don't want to be caught on the roads after dark. There's no telling what dangers might overtake us."

"It's a shame you cannot stay in town for a day or two more." Caroline's mother stood and brushed a bit of lint from the flounce of her wide skirt.

"Now Abigail"—Brother Pierce raised an eyebrow—"we have talked about this at great length. Luke needs to go home and settle Caroline and Mrs. Darby before he has to report back to his unit. There is no time to waste since General Grant seems to have his troops on the move once more."

"You're right, of course." Mrs. Pierce reached for her cloak and drew it around her shoulders. She smiled at her husband, her love for him evident on her face. "It's just so difficult to say good-bye to our little girl."

Brother Pierce patted her shoulder. "She's in good hands." He began moving around the large room, blowing out the candles now that the ceremony was finished.

Tory ran up to where Luke and Caroline stood, threw her arms around her sister, and drew her away from Luke's side as they all gathered their wraps. Luke could hear her excited comments about the beauty of the ceremony as he helped Brother Pierce blow out the remaining candles.

"You will be good to my little girl," said his father-in-law, his voice carrying easily across the empty room. "I agreed to this marriage against my better judgment, you know."

"Yes, sir," Luke responded politely. Inside, he was rather surprised. He'd known Brother Pierce had reservations because of the brevity of their courtship and possibly also because of his rather evasive answers to the reverend's probing spiritual questions. Even though he was a Christian, Luke had not spent much time studying the Bible. He was a good man and felt sure he would go to heaven when he died. That was enough, wasn't it? Especially since he had no desire to don a pair of wings and strum a harp in the afterlife. He'd been baptized when the time was right. Wasn't that what Christ demanded of His followers? "I appreciate your allowing us to be married."

"I went to God with my concerns but could not find in my heart any particular reason to refuse my daughter's wishes. She seems to believe you have a good heart, and I pray you will care for her."

Luke bit down on his tongue to keep from giving the man an abrupt answer. He'd always been taught to respect his elders, but what did Brother Pierce think? That he was going to mistreat Caroline? On the contrary, he could offer her more than most husbands, especially now that he was the owner of Shady Oaks. He had a beautiful home, several hundred acres of crops and woodland, a thriving cane mill, and secure social standing. Caroline would never want for anything. Wasn't that enough? What more did Brother Pierce expect from his son-in-law? "I promise you Caroline will be loved and cared for to the best of my ability." He endured Brother Pierce's direct stare, his chin high.

Finally Brother Pierce nodded and turned toward the carriage where the ladies awaited them.

Luke followed him, feeling somewhat bruised by the older man's inquiry. Apprehension about the future assaulted him, making his heart thump unpleasantly, but Luke pushed it away. He'd made the right choice. His life was finally headed in the right direction. He and Caroline would be a perfect couple—the envy of all who knew them.

eight

"I hope you are not a slugabed." Mrs.—"Grandma Darby" had taken great pleasure in filling their time in the carriage with tales of Shady Oaks Plantation. "Breakfast is served at seven thirty promptly. Anyone who is late will have to wait until noon."

Caroline could not bring herself to say anything, so she nodded her understanding. It was so difficult to think of calling Luke's starchy relative *Grandma*. Calling her Grandmama or Grandmother seemed more fitting. But that is what Luke usually called her, and he insisted she do the same.

"I hope we find everything in order when we get to Shady Oaks." Mrs.—"Grandma Darby" tucked a stray wisp of her graying hair into her chignon. "I told Luke to send a note to the overseer, directing him to have the slaves properly dressed and ready to meet you."

Although she had never been a poor traveler, Caroline was beginning to feel unwell. She had known her new family would own slaves, but she had not considered the reality of treating other human beings like property. She put a hand over her stomach, hoping to calm it.

"You needn't look so disapproving. Your parents have made their abolitionist leanings apparent. I blame people like them for this war." The older woman nodded sharply as though agreeing with herself. "Slaves are a necessary part of running a plantation as large as Shady Oaks. As long as they are not abused, it is a system that benefits both slave and planter.

And we take good care of our slaves. They are practically part of the family."

Caroline refused to argue with her grandmother-in-law before arriving at her new home. She thought of her grandfather Jeremiah LeGrand, who had ended slavery at the plantation in Natchez. Maybe her brother, or even Pa, could give her advice on how to convince Luke and his grandmother to free their slaves and still run a successful plantation.

"You're not much of a talker, are you, girl?"

A headshake was answer enough.

"I declare, I don't know what my grandson sees in you."

Caroline sucked in her breath. "I suppose you'll have to talk to him about that."

"She speaks at last." The older woman's smile did nothing to make Caroline feel better. "I was beginning to think you were either mute or an imbecile with a pretty face."

The carriage slowed before making a sharp turn. Grandma Darby turned her attention to the scenery outside the carriage. "It won't be long now. I can hardly wait to lie down in my own bed."

Caroline wondered if the hotel had not offered comfortable accommodations, but she was not going to ask and have to endure a homily on "The Evils of Staying Away from Home." Not after she'd had to listen to other similar lectures for the past three hours.

If only Luke had ridden inside the carriage, everything would have been different. But he'd decided instead to ride his favorite stallion, Spirit.

It had seemed reasonable this morning when he'd suggested that his two favorite ladies could use the time to get better acquainted. Caroline had even agreed with him. What a mistake that had been. It was only by remembering the warnings in Proverbs about the pitfalls of anger that she had managed to endure the pointed barbs of Luke's grandmother. She prayed Grandma Darby would warm to her once they all settled in at Shady Oaks.

The carriage came to a halt, and Caroline got her first glimpse of her new home. Adjectives like huge, grand, and overwhelming came to mind. Ma's family plantation in Natchez would fit in one corner of this enormous estate. The entrance to the house was some twelve feet above the ground, upheld by a ground floor dotted with narrow windows. A pair of graceful, curved staircases reached upward from the ground to the center of a deep, wide porch boasting a row of whitewashed rocking chairs. Square white columns, at least ten in number, soared from the porch to the roof, supporting a balcony on the second floor that was as wide as the porch below it. The balcony, the porch, and the staircases were encased in black iron railing, another example of the opulence of the estate.

"Oh, my." What had she gotten herself into? Suddenly Caroline understood why her parents had begged her to wait before tying herself to Luke. Why had she not listened to their advice? She could not imagine trying to run such an imposing household.

"I suppose I should not be surprised at your reaction." Luke's grandmother gathered her things as she prepared to get out of the carriage. "I'm beginning to think the reason you don't talk much is because you have very little going on in that mind of yours."

The door opened, and Luke peered in at her. "Welcome to your new home."

Caroline wanted to throw her arms around him and beg him to never leave her alone with his grandmother again. Instead she waited her turn to disembark.

Luke continued holding her hand as he led her up the iron staircase. "I know you and Grandma are weary, but it's important for you to meet your staff before retiring."

It felt good to walk, even though Caroline dreaded having to meet the large group of slaves who had formed a line three people deep that stretched from one end of the front porch to the other. Mostly women, they were a veritable wave of white mobcaps, brown dresses, and white aprons. The men were dressed in brown coats, each with a single row of buttons and a detachable white collar. She felt the weight of their shy glances as her husband led her to the housekeeper, recognizable from the ring of keys she wore at her waist. The woman curtsied as Luke called her name. Caroline smiled and nodded her head while wondering how she would ever keep all their names straight, much less direct their various activities.

Luke didn't stumble a single time, however. He moved from one to the next, patiently telling her the slave's name and area of responsibility. At the end of the line waited a couple whose hands were linked. They were standing a little apart from the others. Caroline knew there must be some significance for their separation from the rest of the staff.

Luke indicated the girl with his hand. "This is Dinah. She'll be your personal maid."

Stifling her immediate discomfort at the idea of a personal servant, much less one who was bound in slavery, Caroline hoped their relationship would instead be one of friendship. She would like to think she would have at least one friend here—besides her husband, of course.

Dinah dropped a quick curtsy, a wide smile betraying her sunny disposition. "Whatever you want, missus, you just tell Dinah about it and I'll take care of it."

"Thank you, Dinah." Caroline wondered if Dinah had a

stash of courage somewhere in the huge mansion.

"And this is Hezekiah. He is both my manservant and Dinah's husband."

Hezekiah bowed. "God bless you, ma'am."

"Thank you, Hezekiah."

"All right, everyone, it's time to get back inside." Luke's grandmother clapped her hands. Caroline had almost forgotten the older woman was outside. "We will expect our supper at the regular time, Mabel."

Which one was Mabel? Ah yes, the short, round woman who had tied a kerchief on her head instead of wearing a cap. She nodded. "I've been cooking all day, ever since Master Luke sent us a note saying all of you was coming home."

"Good." The two women went inside discussing the menu.

Luke took her hand in his. "Are you all right?"

"Yes." She squeezed his large hand, thankful her introduction to the staff was over. "I cannot believe all of those people are slaves."

"Yes, well, I can understand your surprise, but Shady Oaks would not be successful at all if not for their hard labor."

Hand in hand, they walked to the iron rail that framed the porch. A cold wind blew past leafless oak trees and made her shiver.

"Are you cold?"

Caroline shook her head. She wanted to savor this moment with just the two of them. She could and would conquer her fears. "Do you not suppose the plantation could be profitable if you hired people to work in your fields instead of buying slaves?"

The look he tossed her was as cold as the wind buffeting them. "I never want to hear that kind of abolitionist talk from you again, Caroline. You may not realize how tense everyone already is. If you come in here and start fomenting rebellion, we are liable to have our home burned down while we are still abed."

Eager to see love in his eyes instead of the ice now filling them, she nodded.

"Good. That's settled then. We will never speak of it again." He put an arm around her and drew her head onto his shoulder. "Don't disappoint me, Caroline. I have great faith in you, but you will have to adapt to the way we do things here."

After a while she shivered again, and Luke insisted on taking her inside. He made sure Dinah had a warm bath ready for her before leaving his wife in the hands of Hezekiah's wife.

nine

Luke knew he was going to have to do something. Caroline and Grandma had not been getting along all week. He steepled his hands on the surface of his grandfather's walnut desk as he considered his options.

Caroline, sitting on the other side of the desk, was staring at her lap, looking as innocent as a newborn child. Pale winter sunlight slanted into the room from one of the two floor-to-ceiling windows and made her hair gleam, giving the appearance of a golden halo hovering above her head. But he knew his wife was neither as innocent nor as angelic as she appeared.

Instead of using the formal dining room, Caroline was pushing for them to eat dinner at a small table in one of the sitting rooms. Grandma had been scandalized and lost no time in belittling the idea. Neither female was completely right.

While Grandma had been quick to criticize his new wife, Caroline was misguided enough to try the patience of a saint. He wondered why her parents had not been more diligent in teaching her how to manage a proper household. They'd certainly taught her to be diligent in her prayer life, so diligent that he wondered if she loved her Bible more than she loved him.

He understood her need to put her own mark on the household, but Caroline was not being considerate of the established way of doing things at Shady Oaks. His wife seemed determined to change everything from the number of times the family had tea to teaching his slaves stories from the Bible and having them memorize verses. He never would have dreamed his shy, gentle wife would be so full of subversive ideas. "What is the problem now?"

She shook her head. "I don't want to waste your time with trivial matters, Luke. I know you have much more important things on your mind."

"Look at me, Caroline." He waited until she raised her head. He frowned at the puffiness of her eyes. She'd obviously been crying. "I appreciate your consideration of my time, but I cannot get anything done when I have to listen to arguments and complaints all the time. Wouldn't it be easier if you would just go along with Grandma's way of doing things?"

"Yes, but—"

His raised hand stopped her words abruptly. "I don't want to know what the latest problem is. I just want you to go to her and tell her you're sorry Tell her you misunderstood and her way is the right way. Tell her you want to defer to her experience and learn from her. Tell her whatever you need to tell her so that she will not spend another morning talking to me about your lack of consideration."

Her shoulders drooped. Her head hung low.

Luke felt like a beast, but he had to make her understand how to act if he was to get any relief. So many problems awaited his attention. So many solutions had to be worked out before he left, and the time was slipping past him with alarming speed. He did not have time to act as a mediator anymore. His grandmother and his wife were going to have to learn how to live together under the same roof.

"I'm sorry, Luke. I'll try to do as you say." She glanced up at him. "You won't have any more trouble."

He sat back in the leather chair his grandfather had used

to conduct business. He wished Grandpa was still around. Of course that would mean he'd never have come south, never taken over the reins of Shady Oaks, and never married Caroline. Who knew his life would become so complicated so quickly? Would things have been easier if he'd chosen the woman his grandmother had wanted him to marry? Possibly, but it was too late now. He'd made his choice, and they would all have to live with it. Luke rose from his chair and walked around to the front of the desk. "I'll hold you to that promise, dear."

He was ready to give her a hug, but Caroline stood up and, avoiding his gaze, slipped out of the room.

Luke returned to his stack of paperwork with a brief shake of his head. Was it his imagination, or was Caroline hiding something from him?

&

"You won't believe this place." Caroline dragged Dinah down the overgrown path she'd discovered yesterday during a long walk. A walk she'd had to take to keep from exploding at Grandma Darby. She pushed away the uncomfortable memory, along with the memory of not telling her husband about her discovery after she returned to the house and received his lecture. But it was his own fault. He'd not wanted to listen to anything she had to say. All she had done was comply with his wishes.

Dinah tripped over a log lying across the path and would have fallen if not for Caroline's steadying hand. "I don't think we should be out here."

"No one has told me not to come here." Caroline lifted her chin and pulled the maid forward. "If someone finds out, I'll be the one to get in trouble." Not that she could stay out of trouble these days. Who would have ever thought marriage would be so difficult?

She was beginning to be more than a little worried about her husband's faith. Not since they'd arrived had he offered to pray with her or even read scripture to her like Pa did every night. Sunday had come and gone without a mention of the Sabbath. It seemed the only time God was remembered at Shady Oaks was at mealtimes when Luke blessed their food. What had happened to the man who attended every one of her father's revival services?

She'd tried to broach the subject of daily prayer and devotion time with him, but Luke had put her off, saying he had too much to do before he left for Vicksburg. While it was true that he worked from sunup to sundown, she wished he would set aside some time for God. She hoped he meant it when he promised things would get better when the war was over.

"Would you look at that!" Dinah's exclamation brought a smile to her face. "It's a whole empty house."

Dinah was the one bright light at Shady Oaks. From their first evening together, they had discovered they were kindred spirits. It had begun when Dinah shared how she had come to be at Shady Oaks. Caroline knew instinctively this was the first time her new friend had shared such intimate details of her life with someone besides Hezekiah. She knew she could trust Dinah to keep any secrets she might need to share.

Dinah was not sure of her exact age because she'd been sold away from her mother when she was only a babe, but she couldn't be more than five years older than Caroline. She spoke of her good fortune in living at Shady Oaks where she was allowed to marry the man she loved and raise their two children. It humbled Caroline to realize how she took her own freedom for granted.

Caroline let go of her friend's arm and pushed her way

past a wooden gate that had fallen into partial ruin and entered the weed-strewed courtyard. "Come on. I didn't have enough time to explore the inside yesterday."

Dinah's eyes widened. "Do you think somebody lives here?"

"I doubt it." Caroline marched up the front steps and rapped loudly on the door.

Both of them waited breathlessly for a response, but the house remained quiet. No one peeked through any of the windows, most of which were darkened by grimy layers of dirt.

Caroline leaned against the wooden door but heard no footsteps shuffling toward her. "I don't think anyone's been out here in years." She walked over to one of the windows, rubbing at the dirty surface with the hem of her cloak. "I wonder if the original owner of Shady Oaks had this house built, too. It looks like a miniature version of the main house."

Dinah finally joined her on the porch. "I wonder why no one lives here now."

"It's probably too far from the main house to be practical." She looked at Dinah, her mouth forming a perfect *O*. "It might be a dowager house. I wish Luke would move Grandma Darby out here so I wouldn't have to listen to her constant complaints about my failure as a wife."

Dinah's eyes widened.

Caroline took a moment to enjoy the thought before shaking her head. "It would be too mean to exile her out here. I will have to keep praying for a way to please her."

"I've never seen her so unhappy." Dinah's sympathetic gaze raked her face. "I'll pray, too, that she'll be kinder to you."

Fighting to hold back the tears that sprang to her eyes, Caroline turned her attention back to the house. "Let's see if we can get inside. We can clean up one or two of the rooms.

Wouldn't it be wonderful if we could use it to help runaway slaves?"

Dinah's gaze turned dreamy. "You mean like the Underground Railroad?"

"It'd be perfect." Inspiration struck Caroline with the suddenness of a lightning bolt. "I've got it! You and Hezekiah can be the first family we help to escape to a free state."

Dinah froze for a moment before letting her shoulders droop. She shook her head. "My Hezekiah says God put us here for a reason. He'll never run away, and my place is at my husband's side." A tear slid down one of her cheeks. She brushed it away with a finger. "But it's real nice of you to think of us. We don't have a bad life here at Shady Oaks, you know. We have our own house, and your family gives us clothes and food enough to make do. I only have one great dream that will never come to pass."

"What's that?" Caroline tried to put herself in Dinah's place, but it was impossible. She'd always had the support of loving parents and the freedom to do most anything she wanted.

Dinah walked to the edge of the porch and looked back toward the thick woods they'd come through to get here. "Now and again a preacher used to come to Shady Oaks. Master Darby, your husband's grandpa, used to let us come to the chapel when the preacher was here so we could listen to the stories about Jesus. I loved those times, but there hasn't been a preacher stop by since the war started." She turned around to face Caroline. "I know God's Bible is full of stories like the ones he used to tell. But I can't read them. I wish I could so I could share them with my children and my husband."

A yearning to help her friend achieve her dream overcame Caroline. Her excitement returned as a bold idea occurred to her. "That's what we'll do here. We'll have all the privacy in the world, and I can teach you how to read!" She stepped forward and hugged Dinah close. "Let's get inside, and see if there's a place where we can work."

ten

"I'll be back as soon as I can to check on you." Luke gave his wife one last hug. "You be careful. No wandering about alone."

She emerged from his embrace with pink cheeks. "You need to follow your own advice. I'll be perfectly safe here with your grandmother and the staff." Tears filled her eyes, turning them into twin pools. "You're the one who will be risking his life."

Luke felt the tug to stay, but he knew he had no choice. He really should have left two days ago when his orders arrived, but he'd decided to wait until the last possible moment to join the fighting. He would be stationed with a small group of men on one of the bayous between the Yazoo and Mississippi Rivers. His mission was simple—repel any Federal squads trying to reach Vicksburg. "It's much more likely I'll spend my time huddled around a campfire rather than exchanging fire with Yankees."

They walked downstairs arm in arm. "I don't want you to come outside, my darling. It's far too chilly this early." He dropped a kiss on her forehead. "It wouldn't do for you to become ill."

When she would have protested, he covered her mouth with his own. She clung to him and kissed him back. The poignancy of the moment stole his breath. He was glad he'd married her. Glad he would be coming home to her soon.

He pulled away and stared at her beautiful face for several seconds, memorizing the light in her blue eyes, the curve of her chin, the burnished gleam of her golden hair. "I love you."

"I love you, too." The slight catch in her voice was another detail he would carry with him during their separation.

With a sigh he let her go and strode to the front door. Hezekiah was waiting for him, both their horses saddled. "Are all of the provisions ready?"

"Yes, sir. We're all set."

Luke nodded. "You understand you don't have to go with me."

"Yes, sir." Hezekiah swung himself up onto the smaller horse. "I need to go with you. Someone has to protect the master. Your ladies would never recover if something happened to you."

"Thanks, Hezekiah. I appreciate your loyalty." Luke mounted his stallion, and the two of them headed north. If they made good time, they'd arrive at the rendezvous before lunch.

❧

Caroline took her cloak from a hook near the front door.

"Where do you think you're going?" Grandma Darby's voice made her flinch.

"Oh, you startled me." She almost lost her grip on her cloak. "I thought you were in the dining room."

Dressed in a black morning gown, the frowning woman looked like a harbinger of doom. "I finished breaking my fast nearly an hour ago. Since then I've met with the cook, the housekeeper, and the overseer. But none of that answers my question."

"I thought I'd go for a walk." Caroline waited for Grandma Darby to contradict her. In the week since Luke had left, they'd managed to rub along with only a few disagreements, usually caused when Caroline broke some rule she was unaware of.

Grandma opened the front door and looked out. "I think

that's an excellent idea."

Caroline's mouth dropped open. It was the first time Grandma Darby had complimented her choice. After a moment, suspicion wormed its way into her mind. Did she have an ulterior motive?

"I don't think you should go alone, however. Why don't you take Dinah with you?"

Caroline gulped. Had her subterfuge been discovered? Was Luke's grandmother toying with her like a cat with its prey? "Ummm. . .of course. What a good idea." She put her cloak back on the hook. "I'll go find her."

"Don't be silly." Grandma Darby closed the door and moved into the front parlor. "I'll ring for her."

Odd to realize how normal the querulous tone of Luke's grandmother seemed. Her concerns allayed, Caroline hid a smile. She settled on a straight-backed chair in the parlor and waited. A small basket sat at one end of the sofa. She'd never noticed it there before but decided she would follow the adage "Least said, soonest mended."

One of the slaves came running, listened to Grandma Darby's instructions, and hurried off to do her bidding.

A short time later, Dinah stepped into the parlor, an anxious look on her face. She had her cloak draped over one arm.

"Thank you for coming so quickly, Dinah." Caroline ignored Grandma Darby's snort. She was determined to be polite, no matter what the older woman thought. "Shall we get going?"

"I have a favor to ask of you, Caroline."

Grandma Darby's words set her heart thumping once more. She twisted her hands in the folds of her skirt. "What is that?"

"I have a sudden yearning for some sassafras tea, but we don't have any bark in the larder. Do you know what sassafras root looks like?"

Caroline wanted to answer yes, but she could not truthfully do so. "No, ma'am."

Grandma Darby sighed. "Well it's time you do. You'll find a stand of sassafras trees right at the edge of the woods, a few feet to the right of the path that leads to the creek. The roots have a smooth skin, light brown, and very gnarled. You should recognize it by its smell." She turned to glare at Dinah. "You ought to be able to help her."

Dinah's nod eased Caroline's concern. If she knew what a sassafras tree looked like, they could bring Grandma Darby enough roots for a gallon of tea.

Grandma Darby picked up the basket Caroline had noticed earlier. "I asked Cora to ready a basket with a couple of sharp knives. Be careful not to hurt yourself."

As soon as the girls left the house, they began giggling.

Caroline hooked the basket over her arm. "I thought for sure we'd been found out."

"I knew better than that. If Missus Darby found out, she wouldn't have sent word for me to bring my cloak." Dinah's laughter stopped. "I'd more likely be getting a whipping from the overseer."

The very thought made Caroline feel ill. "Maybe we shouldn't go through with this. Maybe I should just teach you the stories. I could read to you. Then you wouldn't be at risk of such a severe punishment."

Dinah planted her feet on the path and both hands on her hips. "Are you saying you don't want to teach me to read?"

"No, no. Not at all." Caroline could hear the strain in her voice. "My only concern is you, Dinah. You're the one who'll have to pay the price if we're ever caught."

"I suppose we'd better not get caught." Dinah resumed walking. "I think the good Lord knows what we're doing and why, and He'll protect us."

Caroline felt humbled by her words. "Sometimes I think you've got more faith than I do."

Dinah shook her head. "We're both God's children, and that's all that matters." She paused at the edge of the woods. "Do you want to pick the sassyfras now or when we're coming back?"

"Let's do it after your lesson. That way the roots will be nice and fresh. I don't want to give Grandma Darby any more reason to complain."

They arrived at the deserted house without incident and settled in for a lesson. Caroline was watching Dinah copy her letters on a piece of stationery. "Yes, that's a—" Her words were cut off by an eerie sound.

"What's that?" Dinah's eyes widened.

"I don't know." Caroline kept her voice to a whisper.

"Sounds like it's coming from out back."

Caroline had her hearing stretched to maximum. "It almost sounds like a baby crying." She got up and crept down the shadowy hallway leading to the back porch. She nearly jumped out of her skin when something touched her arm. Whirling around, she found Dinah right behind her. "You scared me half to death."

"Sorry." Dinah held out one of the knives from Grandma Darby's basket. "I thought we might need these."

"Good idea." Caroline crept forward again. It was quiet for a moment or two, but then the sound returned. It did sound like a baby. But what would a baby be doing out here in the woods? Had someone set up housekeeping?

"It can't be a baby." Dinah held her knife out in front of her.

Caroline had a firm grip on her weapon, but she held it at her side. "What could it be then?"

"Maybe it's a deserter trying to draw us outside where he can rob us. . . ." Her voice faded away into nothingness.

"Maybe we ought to leave while we can."

Caroline turned back to look at Dinah. She squared her shoulders and lifted her chin. "I'm not going to run away like a coward." She stopped whispering, but her voice was still a little shaky. "This is my home. As long as Luke isn't here, it's my responsibility to make sure we're protected."

Dinah's eyes were as wide as saucers. "Or we could go back out the front way and get help."

It was tempting to listen to Dinah's suggestion, but Caroline knew in her heart she could not shirk her duty. She might not know much about running a plantation like Shady Oaks, but she ought to be able to scare off a vagrant before he caused any trouble.

Caroline looked at Dinah as she pulled the back door open and stepped out onto the narrow porch. "No, there's no time. But you stay inside. If I don't come back in a few minutes, you run back to the big house and bring the overseer back here as fast as you can manage."

"Stay in here? By myself? While you go out there and get yourself killed. . .or worse? I can't do that."

Caroline didn't answer. Her attention was on the grounds behind the house and the line of trees several yards back. She could see some evidence the area immediately behind the house had been cleared at some point in the past, even noticing the outline of what had to be an old flower garden. Lack of attention, however, had given nature the chance to reclaim most of the yard with weeds, creeping vines, and thorny bushes.

The noise came again, and from where she stood, it sounded even more like a baby crying. She caught a movement from the corner of her eye and whipped her head around to see a dark shape prowling among the trees at the edge of the woods. She held her breath. The figure weaved in and out of the brush, indistinct even in the bright morning light. Finally she made out its shape. It was a large, obviously anxious animal. As she watched, the coal-black shape leaped to a branch that had to be at least ten feet above the ground. Her breath caught at the grace of the smooth move, and she knew it to be a cat. . .a large cat. It made her think of the caged lions she had seen the year her parents had visited a traveling circus in Natchez. Except this animal was as black as midnight.

"Can you see anything yet?" Dinah had joined her on the porch. "What is it? Is it a deserter?"

"Shh. . .no, it's not a deserter. I think it's a cat."

"A cat? Like a housecat?"

"No, more like a lion." She pointed to the shadowy branches where it had taken refuge. "See, up there. Its fur is so black I almost can't make it out, but if you look real close, you can see its green eyes shining."

"It must be a panther." Dinah's voice was calmer now.

"A panther? I've heard about those, but I've never seen one."

"They're secretive."

"This one doesn't seem to be very secretive. I wonder why it's staying so close to the house even though it knows we're here."

"It's come to eat us up, that's what."

"Don't be silly, Dinah. Panthers don't eat people." Caroline's heart sped up a notch. Did they?

"I've heard stories of big cats that can sneak into a baby's room and take him away before anybody knows what's happening. They said it happened a few years back over at the Devereaux place. The next morning, the mother went to get her poor baby and it was gone. The only thing left in the crib was a few drops of blood and a patch of fur as black as night."

Caroline shuddered. She'd never heard of a panther taking

a baby, but maybe it happened to people who lived so far from civilization. Just then the noise that had attracted their attention in the first place returned. It was much closer than the panther sitting so quietly on the tree limb. It seemed to come from right beneath her feet.

Dinah must have heard it, too, because she grabbed Caroline's free hand and squeezed it tight.

At least they knew it wasn't a deserter. But Caroline was beginning to wonder if the true answer was going to be even more dangerous. "What do you think is making that noise?"

Dinah looked at her. "Do you think it could be a baby panther?"

She nodded. "That's what I think, too. But I wonder where it is."

"There may be a root cellar. You know, where the missus of this place kept her canned fruits and vegetables."

Caroline glanced around the overgrown yard. What Dinah was saying made sense. A young cub could have somehow managed to get itself trapped, and that would be its mother out there, waiting to see what they were going to do.

"We'll have to find it," Caroline said. "The mother obviously can't help it, so we'll have to free the cub."

"What if it's not a cub at all?" asked Dinah. "What if it's the father panther, and we get eaten up when we find him?"

The noise started again. "I don't see any way that could be a full-grown panther. It's got to be a baby crying for its mother."

Although the look on Dinah's face was still full of doubt and fear, she took a deep breath and nodded her agreement.

"Good." Caroline pointed to her right, away from the area where the panther watched from the woods. "You start over there, and I'll start on this side of the yard. Just be careful to stay away from the woods. We don't want her to feel threatened. I'd hate to try to outrun her."

The two women stepped off the porch and searched quietly in the yard. Several tense moments passed before Caroline spied a pair of old wooden doors that looked like they were lying on the ground. "I think I've found it."

She moved closer and noticed that the wood on the doors was weathered. She could even see a wide gap where one of the boards had rotted away. This must be where the young cub had gotten in trouble. He'd probably just been exploring when the old board gave way underneath him. The space was far too small for the mother panther to get in and rescue her baby.

Caroline could hear the frightened yowls clearly now. She looked over her shoulder in time to see the mother panther standing on the branch, watching every move she made. The animal's wail sent shivers chasing down her spine. Caroline wondered whether the sound was to calm the little one or to warn her away.

Dinah walked over, her face showing a mixture of relief and fear. "Did you hear that?"

"Yes, but she's still out there in the woods. I hope she's trying to calm her cub."

"What do we do now?"

Caroline studied the area around them. "We've got to find a way to open those doors."

The cries from the other side of the doors were louder now and continued without pause. Caroline wondered if they should abandon the cub to its fate. It would certainly be the easier answer. But she knew she couldn't live with herself if she didn't try to do something to help the poor animal. She wanted to send Dinah back inside to safety but knew it was unlikely the other woman would desert her. With a nod to the mother cat, she bent over and grabbed the wooden handle on one of the doors, pulling with all her might. It didn't budge.

"Here, let me help." Dinah leaned over and grabbed the wooden edge just above Caroline's hands.

The two women pulled and strained. Caroline was beginning to believe they would not be able to get the door open when the old hinges groaned and began to give way. With renewed strength, the two women redoubled their efforts and were rewarded when the door opened fully. The second door didn't give them as much trouble, opening as if its hinges had been more faithfully oiled. Or perhaps their renewed hope gave them extra strength.

Dinah took two steps back. "Are you going down in there?"

"Why else did we work so hard to get the doors open?"

"I don't know." Dinah glanced toward the woods. "Maybe we could just leave it like this and let the mother come rescue her cub."

Caroline shook her head. "What if the poor thing is hurt?"

"We can't do anything if it is."

"I cannot stand here and let that baby cry. It could be hours before the mother feels it's safe enough to come this close to the house." Caroline took a step down into the cellar. It was dark, but not nearly as musty or dank as she imagined it might be. In fact, it had a rather pleasant smell, as if someone had used the cellar to dry herbs.

Three steps took her to the well-packed earthen floor, and she waited for her eyes to adjust to the gloom. It was a small room, bare of furniture except for a table and bench in one corner. After a moment she also noticed the shelves lining the other three walls. Most of the shelves were empty, but here and there she could see jars still packed with fruits or vegetables. The panther cub had quieted when she entered the cellar, so Caroline had no idea where to look for the animal.

"Do you see it?" Dinah's voice seemed far away.

Caroline's gaze searched the gloomy room. "No, not yet."

She leaned over the bench. Emerald-green eyes peered at her from under the table, eyes as bright as those of its concerned mother outside. "Oh wait, here it is. Come here, little cat. I'm going to take you to your mother." She approached the cub slowly, unsure of its reaction, and held her hand out in what she hoped was an unthreatening gesture.

"Be careful, Miss Caroline."

Caroline jumped at Dinah's hoarse voice. A giggle tried to work its way up her throat, but she fought it. This was no time to get hysterical.

Something wet brushed the fingers she had extended. It took every ounce of determination she had not to jump back as the panther cub sniffed cautiously. Then it rubbed its head against her fingers, and she felt its soft fur tickling her skin.

"There, there. I know you're scared, little fellow." Her voice was calmer than she would have thought possible. It must be the touch of God's grace. Gaining more self-assurance as the animal allowed her to stroke its head and neck, she closed the distance between them. "Why don't you come here and let me help you get back to your ma? I know you must be missing her something awful. And aren't you a smart kitten to make such a noise?"

A low, rumbling sound issued from the young panther's throat, and it butted its head against her hand. She had gained its trust.

"That's it, little fellow." She carefully picked up the cat and held it in the crook of her arm. The cub rubbed its head against her arm, apparently content to let her carry it away from the dark corner where it had taken refuge. She walked back up the stairs and into the daylight.

"Praise the Lord." Dinah's admiration was plain to see. "You got him."

"Can you see the mother cat?" Caroline peered toward the woods.

"She's over there now." Dinah pointed to a clump of bushes and weeds. "She jumped down from her perch about the time you went into the cellar. She hasn't moved any closer to the house, so I hope she's not planning to attack us."

"I rather doubt that, or she would have done it by now." Caroline looked down at the ebony cat. "Look at this little fellow. Isn't he adorable?"

"If you say so, Miss Caroline." Dinah didn't look convinced. "But you'd better put him down before he decides to start crying again. I don't like the idea of you holding a wild animal, especially since its anxious ma is standing right over there."

"I will, but I need to pick a good spot. A place far enough away from us so his mother can come and see about him. And far enough from the cellar doors that he won't get into trouble again." She looked around, remembering the old flower garden. It should be a safe place to set down the adventurous cub. "I'll take you over there, little guy, and then Dinah and I will wait to make sure your ma comes to get you."

While Caroline walked slowly across the yard, Dinah closed the root cellar doors. "I'm going to wait for you on the back porch."

Caroline nodded. She continued petting the cub as if he were a housecat. As she approached the garden area, she could hear movement in the grass behind her. "It's probably your ma come to get you." Her heart pounded, but she kept walking forward with even, measured steps.

When she reached the garden, she carefully placed the cub on the ground and turned around, her breath catching in her throat. The mother panther was only a few yards away. She took a step to her right, hoping the mother would see she had not harmed the cub.

Although the animal was poised as if to spring, she didn't move. Her bright-green gaze followed Caroline's movements until she was a few feet closer to the house. Then she transferred her attention to the cub, which was unhurriedly licking its front paw.

Caroline continued her slow movements backward, praying she would not fall over an obstacle. After what seemed an eternity, she bumped up against the back porch. Safety was within reach. She moved up the stairs, keeping her attention glued to the panthers.

The mother panther walked over to the cub and sniffed him. She put out a large paw and pushed the cub onto his back, sniffing its stomach. Then she used her head to push the cub back onto his feet. Apparently satisfied, she grabbed the cub by the scruff of his neck and began to walk toward the woods.

Caroline breathed a sigh of relief as mother and babe returned to the wilderness where they belonged. She felt a great deal of satisfaction in knowing she could stand her ground. With God's help, she could overcome her fears and doubts, conceive a plan, and make it work. Maybe one day she would be able to take on the duty and responsibility of running Shady Oaks. Perhaps she could even improve things on the plantation. With the grace of God, she could do some good in this little corner of the world.

"Come on inside." Dinah stood at the back door.

"I'll be there in a minute." Caroline wasn't sure why she wanted to remain out here on the porch. The cub was safe. Dinah was safe. She was safe. But she stood caught up in a sense of wonder, watching the powerful, graceful movements of the big cat as she loped away.

Just before the panther disappeared into the woods, she turned, the cub still dangling from her jaws. Those piercing green eyes looked at her, and Caroline felt a chill dance across her skin. For a moment she felt the full force of the panther's stare. Was she grateful to Caroline? It might be a fanciful idea, but in her heart she knew she and the mother panther had connected on some level.

God's hand was in the events of the afternoon. Besides the remarkable coincidence that the cub had picked this day to fall into the root cellar, it amazed her to think that they had been able to hear the cub all the way from the root cellar. And the mother panther had never threatened them, even though she was a fearsome creature with teeth and claws that could have easily torn them to shreds.

God, You are so awesome. You used this encounter to teach me to rely on Your strength. A feeling of tranquility filled her heart, just like the peace beyond man's understanding that Paul promised in his letter to the Philippians. No longer did she feel all alone in facing her problems. Regardless of the circumstances surrounding them, God would see them through each day.

eleven

Luke took a deep breath and raised his left hand. His right held a loaded pistol. His rifle lay beside him on the limb of the cottonwood in which he perched. He waited for the precise moment of attack, every muscle in his body tense as he watched the enemy soldiers mucking their way across the shallow bayou. Closer, closer, closer. . .With the lethal swiftness of a striking copperhead, his arm fell.

Simultaneously four shots rang out in the predawn gloom. Four Yankees fell into the water, leaving the men behind them, still wading in water above their knees, at a disadvantage. They reached for their weapons, but it was already too late. Luke led the second volley with his rifle. Shouts and screams of confusion and pain filled the area. The icy water of the little river was turning red with the blood of the fallen men.

In between his small troop and the river, some cattails rustled and shook. Luke heard the *whoosh* of a breath and a quiet splash. The pointed snout of an alligator headed for the wounded and dying men, its keen sense of smell leading it unerringly toward a floating body.

When the surviving men in the river saw the gray shape swimming toward them with deadly intent, they broke rank. It was one thing to face the chance of catching a bullet, quite a different danger to become breakfast for a voracious reptile. They pushed each other out of the way in their haste to escape. After a few minutes, the sounds of their retreat had faded into the distance.

Luke reloaded before he signaled to the others to join him on the riverbank. His face was frozen into a grim mask. He hated this—ambushing unsuspecting men, the death, the thrashing of gators as they completed their grisly feeding.

For nearly a month his days had been filled with too much death and destruction. How he longed for a respite, for the sweet smell of fresh earth and the new cane that should have sprouted by now. Even in the swamp, the signs of spring were all around them. The oak trees and hickory trees had put on their new leaves, bringing to mind his grandfather's words about planting various crops. He must have known even then that his grandson would one day need the information. *"The smart farmer plants corn when the leaves of a hickory tree get as big as a squirrel's ear."*

Those days were long gone, the happy memories fading as the horrors of war filled Luke's heart and mind. The world had become a wicked place. He hoped Shady Oaks was still untouched. He needed to believe he could one day return to the security of hearth and home. Once again feel the steady gait of his powerful stallion, Spirit, as they toured the fields. Hug his wife and tell her how much he loved her.

Luke stretched his senses to their most sensitive, listening for the return of the Union soldiers. He didn't expect it, but he must remain alert as an officer might manage to turn the troops around and send them back in this direction. He heard nothing but the croak of a bullfrog, the calls of birds, and the slap of water against the bank.

He walked over to where one of the bodies not mangled by the gator lay. Two of them lay lifeless on the riverbank, the blue of their uniforms turning black in the water. His foot flipped the nearest body. The face that stared up at him looked so young, so innocent. Surely this soldier was younger than sixteen. A hollow feeling invaded his stomach. His eyes stung, and his breath came in ragged gasps.

"Look out!" Hamp's urgency broke through the misery.

Hands shoved him hard, and Luke fell to one knee. He twisted and pulled his gun, shooting by instinct. Two blasts rent the air.

The other wounded soldier fell back, dead before his body hit the ground.

Time seemed to stretch as Luke straightened. He felt that he was moving through air as thick as syrup. Horror overtook him when he saw Hampton swaying behind him, staring with some surprise at a dark stain on the front of his uniform.

"I believe you owe me a favor, old man." Hamp sat down on the muddy bank with a thump.

Luke reached out to catch him. "No, no. You can't be hit."

"Sorry to argue with a commanding officer"—Hamp coughed and groaned—"but I rather think I am."

"Hezekiah! Come quick!" Luke jerked the tail of his shirt free of his pants and tore off a wide strip of lawn. With quick motions, he folded it into a square and pressed it against the hole in Hamp's chest.

The large black man splashed across the bayou. "What happened?"

"We've got to get Hamp to town. There'll be a surgeon there."

Hamp coughed. "I—it's too late."

Luke turned back to his friend. "You're going to be okay. You have to be."

"Wrong again."

"Don't argue with me. Save your strength." Luke's voice was rough. He looked up. "Get something to bind the wound. A belt, a piece of rope, anything." He continued applying pressure to the awful wound, even though he could feel the blood seeping through the material.

Hamp's green eyes were dull and seemed fixed on an object behind Luke's shoulder. "It's all right. My soul will be free to join God."

"Amen." Hezekiah handed a frayed rope to Luke. He continued whispering under his breath, and Luke assumed he was praying. He wished he could think of the right words to pray for God to work a miracle.

It was all over in minutes. Luke continued to hold his friend until Hamp's body went limp. Tears of regret, anger, and frustration rolled down his face. When would the senseless killing end?

Gently Hezekiah leaned forward and pulled Hamp's body away from him. "We need to get out of here."

Luke nodded. Any moment the enemy soldiers could return. Then they'd all die. He allowed Hezekiah to lift Hamp's body over his broad shoulder. Luke picked up all the rifles strewed about on the ground, and they made their way across the forest to the camp. After directing the other men to pack up the camp and follow them to Vicksburg, Luke and Hezekiah saddled their horses and left.

The tall spire of a church appeared over the rise of a hill. "They deserve to know Hampton died a hero." Guilt squeezed his chest as he looked back over his shoulder.

"You don't need to feel like that, Master Luke. That Yankee soldier is the one who pulled the trigger."

"But if I'd been paying attention, that soldier wouldn't have had a chance to get a shot off at poor old Hamp."

"Every man's got to die, and it's the good Lord who decides when."

Luke wanted to yell at his slave, but he settled for bitterness. "Don't talk to me about a God who would allow this senseless killing to go on. Hamp was a good man. He didn't deserve to die."

"Maybe God wanted Master Hamp at *His* side." The black man didn't flinch under the heat of Luke's glare.

"All I know is Hamp hasn't even had time to really fall in love or father his own children. Why did Hamp die? Why am I still alive? I'm no better than he is. . .was."

"I don't know what you want to hear, Master Luke. The good Lord is the only One who knows why this one lives and that one dies."

Anger threatened to consume him. It felt like a physical wound, as if he was the one who had been shot. He wanted to kick his stallion to a gallop. The need to feel the wind blowing past him was almost overwhelming. Was he trying to outrun his guilt? Luke didn't know. He only knew that nothing made sense anymore.

♦

Caroline couldn't quell the feeling of unease. Was it the weather? Relentless rain dripped from the eaves of the main house. She and Dinah had not been able to return to the house in the woods for more than a week. Maybe that was the reason for her restlessness. She sighed and put her needlework in the basket at her feet. Rising from the sofa, she drifted toward the window and stared out at the gray afternoon. Summer couldn't come soon enough for her liking.

At least she and Grandma Darby were getting along better. Even though she felt it was silly for the two of them to eat in the spacious dining room at the huge table, she held her tongue and endured the formal meals. It was not too high a price to pay in the name of peace. The Lord had answered her prayers about the stilted relationship between her and Luke's grandmother. Since the day Grandma Darby asked for sassafras root, things had gotten better. Caroline and Dinah had dug up the gnarled roots and carried them back to Cora. That very afternoon, Grandma Darby had been served sassafras tea made from the pungent roots. Caroline was trying to acquire a taste for it.

A rustle behind her made Caroline turn. "Good morning, Grandma Darby."

The older woman frowned. "I don't see what's so good about it. We've had enough rain to drown ducks."

Caroline had a hard time keeping her expression solemn. "Well, I suppose we should give thanks for having such a lovely home to keep us safe and warm."

"And what about the soldiers who are not so blessed?" Grandma Darby stalked to the fireplace and held her hands out to the warmth. "It must be miserable for poor Luke and the others. I pray they have found a warm, dry place for shelter."

Even though she tried to ignore it, the dark feeling of foreboding grew stronger. "I wonder when we will hear from Luke."

The words were no sooner out of her mouth than a clamor started in the central hallway. She turned toward the door. Hope it was her husband arriving, no matter how unrealistic that might be, replaced the dread in her heart. She looked out the window for sight of Luke or his stallion. Her eyes widened. A group of black men stood on the front lawn, wearing ragged clothing and angry expressions. "Whatever is going on?"

"Who is it?" Grandma Darby came to stand next to her. "Slaves? I don't recognize any of them."

At that moment, the door to the parlor opened and Dinah hurried in. "I'm sorry, missus. There's some men outside, and they're threatening to burn us out if we don't give 'em what they want."

Grandma Darby gasped. "Burn us out?" What little color

she'd had in her face drained away. She put a hand to her forehead and swayed.

Caroline slipped a hand around her waist and helped her reach the sofa. "You sit here a moment and. . ." She let her words fade. What was she going to do? Face an angry mob? What would she say? How could she keep them from carrying out their threats?

Stories of violent slave uprisings returned to haunt her. Were they all about to die? She glanced at Dinah, whose eyes were as large as they had been the day they'd rescued the baby panther. The memory of that day steadied her somehow. God had helped her then. He would be faithful to stand by her today.

She took a deep breath and sent a prayer heavenward for courage and wisdom. "I'll be back soon, Grandma Darby. Dinah, why don't you see if you can brew up some of that sassafras tea? By the time I get done with the men out front, we'll probably all need a little refreshment."

Dinah scurried off to do her bidding while Caroline headed toward the main foyer. She could hear the strident yells of the men outside, but so far the Darby slaves had not allowed any of them to come into their home.

She pointed to two of the older footmen. "I need you to stand behind me while I speak with our visitors."

The men glanced at each other before turning to follow her. Good. At least now she could give the appearance of authority. She reached for the front door, but one of the footmen stepped past her and opened it, bowing as she passed through the opening.

The temperature was warmer than she expected, but the dampness seeped into her bones. Ignoring the physical discomfort, she stared out over the group of about twenty men. "I understand you men need some supplies."

"That's right." One man, apparently the leader, stood on the topmost step. "We're on our way to join up with the Union army, and we need food and blankets. If you're not gonna give 'em to us, we're gonna take 'em."

Caroline didn't answer him right away. Instead she looked at the men behind him, allowing time to meet each man's gaze. "So you're going to make war on a couple of women?" She continued to focus on each of the faces, ignoring the leader's growl. Their faces turned from anger to shame as she continued staring.

"Why not?" The leader took a step up, his foot landing squarely on the wooden planks of the front porch. "You got enough to share with us, and then some." He looked her up and down.

Everything in her wanted to turn and run. And she might have done it if her feet had not been nailed to the floor. But she couldn't run. She had to stand up to the man and win out. Squaring her shoulders and raising her chin, she faced him down. "We are more than willing to share with you if you're willing to be calm and respectful. But if you continue to threaten me and my family, I'll see to it that you're run off this property without so much as a biscuit to eat."

His eyes widened in surprise. For a moment, she could sense the struggle within him. She prayed hard for the Lord to protect her, to breathe a spirit of conciliation into the man. His gaze dropped to the floor at his feet, and he nodded. "Yes, ma'am."

Relief swept through her like a spring flood. "That's fine then." She smiled at the group of men, further relieved when one or two of them returned her smile. "Why don't all of you go around to the kitchen. Our cook, Cora, will see to your immediate needs while we gather some fresh clothing and food for you."

She turned on her heel and swept back toward the door without watching to see if they would follow her instructions. Praises filled her mind. She swept inside on a tide of thanksgiving. Disaster had been averted. Wouldn't Ma and Pa be shocked to see how she'd stood up to the unruly group? And Luke. Would he be impressed?

Seeing Mabel, who had probably come after hearing the clamor, Caroline asked her to gather the promised items for the men. She then turned to join Grandma Darby, who met her at the entrance to the parlor.

Pulling her into a tight embrace, Grandma Darby said, "I'm so glad Luke chose you to be his wife. I don't know many women brave enough to confront runaway slaves."

As soon as she emerged from the embrace, Caroline smiled. "It wasn't me, you know. It was God. Without His presence, I wouldn't have known how to act or what to say. God changed the heart of their leader. I saw it happen, Grandma Darby. It was amazing."

"I'm sure it was." Grandma Darby led her to the sofa. Both of them sat down, their hands entwined. "And I don't know what you must think of me. A foolish old lady who was no help at all."

Caroline shook her head. "Don't even think such a thing. You know more about this plantation than I'll ever know. All of the details come naturally to you, but they make my head swim. What I did was nothing in comparison. If I had not been here, you would have managed. On the other hand, I could never manage without your knowledge and guidance."

Tears swam in the older woman's eyes, making them gleam. "I don't know why I've been so blind. Can you ever forgive me, Caroline?"

Leaning forward, she placed a kiss on Grandma Darby's soft cheek. "Only if you'll forgive me for my lack of sense."

Grandma Darby let go of her hands and hugged Caroline once again. "There's nothing to forgive, Granddaughter."

Someone knocked on the door.

"Come in," they said simultaneously. Their gazes met, and they broke into giggles.

Dinah walked in with a laden tray. "Are you ready for some tea?"

Caroline nodded, trying unsuccessfully to stop her giggles. She supposed it was a reaction to her fear. She really should go to the kitchen out back and oversee the provisions being given to the visitors. But she wanted to enjoy the new closeness with her grandmother-in-law.

Grandma Darby looked from the tray to Caroline. "You even thought to order a tray? I think you're going to make a fine mistress of Shady Oaks."

twelve

Luke could not believe he was about to attend a rally for the troops. Call it what they would, he knew it was nothing more than an opportunity for the citizens to enjoy another evening of dancing and flirting. He could list a thousand reasons why he should not. He'd just lost a close friend. Yankee soldiers were closing in on Vicksburg. And the obvious—he was married.

Hezekiah fussed with his cravat. "I don't know about this, Master Luke. What would your grandma say about this?"

He twisted his chin away from the black man's fingers. "She'd probably say I deserved a night of leisure after all I've been through." Even though he was looking away from Hezekiah, Luke could feel the large man's frown. He hunched a shoulder.

"She would think it's honorable for you to be seeing another woman?"

Hezekiah's firm jerk on the cravat made Luke cough and gasp for breath. "Careful."

"I'm sorry, Master Luke." Hezekiah twisted the length of cotton into some complicated design before stepping back. "It's done now."

It might have been the disappointed look in the other man's eyes. Or it might have been the voice of conscience. Either way, it made Luke very uncomfortable and not a little defensive. "Don't raise such smoke over this. It's not like I'm going to be alone with some female. I'm only going to a dance. Everything will be aboveboard and open to public scrutiny. I would never break my vows."

"Christ said we have to stay clean all the way through. It's not good enough to appear to be good. Just thinking about doing something sinful is as bad as actually doing it."

Luke snorted and pushed himself up from his dressing table. "If that were really true, we'd all be lost without hope."

Hezekiah's smile was sad and yet full of wisdom. "That's why we need Christ. Without Him, not even one of us could look forward to everlasting life."

Luke mulled over Hezekiah's words as he finished dressing. It didn't make sense. Why would God make it so impossible for men to get to heaven? Why would He make men so fallible they were sure to fail? "Do you think Hampton is in heaven now?"

"I don't rightly know, Master Luke. Only the good Lord knows what's in a man's soul."

"What about you, Hezekiah? Are you going to go to heaven when you die?"

Hezekiah put down the frock coat he'd been brushing. "Well, yes sir, I am. But I'm not in any special hurry. I love my family, and I'd like to live long enough to see my children placed in good homes."

The gentle tone in Hezekiah's voice awoke something in Luke. It was a yearning. A desire to be like the man who was carefully folding his clothing.

He shook his head to clear it. What was he thinking? He wanted to be like his slave? A man who didn't have any control over his life or the lives of his children? What foolishness. He was a successful man, a man others envied. He had a beautiful wife, a thriving plantation, and an idyllic future. By anyone's standards, he was a man who had everything. "I'm glad you're not in a hurry to get to heaven." He clapped Hezekiah on the back. "I'm not ready for you to leave me behind."

Hezekiah smiled. "Thank you, Master Luke."

Luke checked his reflection in the mirror before leaving his room. He was ready to enjoy an evening of music and dancing.

❧

"I was so glad to see you here, Luke." Marianna's dark eyes gleamed as he whirled her around on the dance floor.

Luke wondered why he hadn't chosen this young lady to be his bride. If only he could go back in time, that's one thing he would change. The other being his failure to stop Hampton from being killed. "I only wish I was here under happier circumstances."

Her mouth turned down at the corners. "I heard about Mr. Boothe. We will miss him terribly."

"Yes." He kept his answer short. No need to go into detail. He wasn't sure he could tell her what had happened without breaking down and making a fool of himself. "What's been going on in Vicksburg since I left?"

Her sad expression disappeared like a discarded mask. "Geraldine Stringer and Phillip Anderson announced their engagement. They will get married in August." Her sly glance was full of mischief. "Not everyone is as anxious as you to tie the knot."

"And rightly so. If I had to do it again. . ." He let the words trail off. Marianna was smart enough to understand his implication.

Her cheeks turned pink, and she looked past his shoulder. "I have been busy myself." The words were spoken in an offhand manner, as though her attention was elsewhere.

A little peeved at her inattention, he swung her around so she would have to focus on him. . .or at least on her dance steps. "Are you still volunteering your time with the soldiers?"

"Yes. It's hard, but rewarding at the same time." Her

answer sounded stilted to him. As though she was answering him by rote. She felt stiffer, too. Was she no longer comfortable dancing with him?

Before he could ask if he had offended Marianna in some way, the music ended. He escorted her back to her mother and watched as one of his commanding officers, Major Fontenot, approached.

Swarthy-skinned with a mustache thicker and wider than Luke's, he looked like a pirate of old. All he needed was a black eye patch and an open-throated shirt. "Good evening. I hope you have not turned Miss Lister's head with too many compliments."

Why did the man's voice grate on him? Luke gave him a tight smile. "I don't believe I could."

"*Excusez-moi.* I stand corrected." Major Fontenot raised an eyebrow as he made a show of looking around the crowded ballroom. "How is your lovely bride? I have not seen her this evening."

"She is not here." Luke could feel anger building in his chest. Who did Fontenot think he was?

A married man.

The voice in his head was quiet, but he heard it in spite of the noise around him.

The snap of Marianna's fan opening drew his attention. She smiled at him. "Captain Talbot brought poor Mr. Boothe back to his parents."

Luke could almost hear the other man's questions. Why was he here tonight? Why hadn't he gone home right after meeting with the Boothe family? Why had he chosen to attend a party instead of flying to his wife when he had an opportunity?

Suddenly Luke wondered the same things. What was he doing here?

While he was still lost in contemplation, Fontenot led Marianna to the ballroom floor. He watched them twirl around the room for a few moments, surprised to see how she glowed.

He thought of the way Caroline looked at him. Perhaps he could make a quick trip to Shady Oaks if he got up very early in the morning. He would have to return again tomorrow evening, but being near her for even an hour or two would make the trip worth his effort.

Having made up his mind, Luke took his leave and headed back to his room. He would need to be up before the sun in the morning.

thirteen

"Are you going walking again?" Grandma Darby's voice stopped Caroline and Dinah at the threshold to the front porch.

Caroline hesitated. She didn't like deceiving the older woman, but it was true they were going to walk to the dowager house. "Yes, ma'am." She hoped God would forgive her for not being any more specific about their plans. She turned back to the parlor to find both Grandma Darby and the housekeeper in the cozy room. "Do you need us to gather anything for you while we're outside?"

"No, I think we have everything we need for the moment." Grandma Darby looked toward Mabel. "You're not aware of anything, are you?"

"No, ma'am."

Grandma Darby nodded, turning her attention back to Caroline. "Please be sure to take Dinah with you. After what happened the other day, we should be doubly careful about not venturing out alone."

Caroline leaned forward and kissed Grandma Darby's cheek. "Don't worry about us. We'll be very careful." It was at times like these she wanted to confess exactly where she and Dinah would be and what they would be doing, but even though her relationship with Luke's grandmother was better, she doubted the woman would understand why she was determined to teach Dinah how to read and write. That was a secret she would have to keep for a very long time.

❧

Luke jumped down from his horse and tossed the reins to

one of the stable boys who had come running to the front of the house. He could hardly wait to see Caroline. He had so much to talk to her about. And he wanted to hear every detail of all she had been doing since he left.

Would she have managed a truce with Grandma? Or were the two of them still feuding over insignificant differences? A smile curved his lips. He was almost looking forward to the role of peacemaker.

He took the steps two at a time and pushed open the front door. Pulling off his cloak, he laid it across an ornate bench inside the entry hall. "Caroline? Grandma?" He glanced in the parlor, but it was empty.

A sound from the top of the staircase brought his head up. Expecting to see one or both of the women, he was disappointed to recognize the housekeeper. "Mabel, where is everyone?"

The woman hurried down the stairs. "Your grandmother is in her room resting, and your wife has gone out walking."

"Walking?" He scratched his head. "Isn't it too cold to be outside?"

A shrug answered his question. "Not for her and her maid, it's not. The two of them usually spend every morning out in the woods. But don't you worry. They'll probably be back before too long. They rarely miss lunch."

Luke's spirits deflated. He'd been so excited about surprising them. All the way home he'd imagined the joy on Caroline's face when he arrived. But now she wasn't even here. He glanced around the open entryway and sighed. What would he do until she appeared? Waiting seemed like an unacceptable pastime.

An idea formed in his head. Maybe he wouldn't have to wait. "Which way did they go?"

Mabel inclined her head over her left shoulder. "They

generally use that path on the far side of the smokehouse."

Grabbing his cloak from the bench, Luke nodded. "I bet I know exactly where I'll find them."

&

Dinah was leaning over a scrap of newspaper, her finger tracing the outline of the next word in the title she was trying to read.

"What is the first letter?" Caroline coaxed her student.

"G. . .G. . .ran. . .t. . .Grant!" She looked up for confirmation.

"That's right. Grant. And the next word?"

"F. . .fails. Ag. . .again. 'Grant Fails Again.'"

"Very good, Dinah. Look at that. You're reading the newspaper."

They were so excited neither of them heard the footsteps on the porch. The first indication they had they were not alone was the sound of a deep voice. "That's a hanging offense."

"Luke!" Caroline jumped up from her seat next to Dinah. Excitement and fear fought for supremacy in her mind. One glance at his face was all it took for the fear to win out. He was angrier than she'd ever seen him. "Luke." The second time she said his name, it was a plea for understanding.

He took off his gray cap and slapped it against the stripe on his pants leg, his dark gaze boring into Dinah's frightened face. He jerked his chin up and slightly back. "Get yourself to the big house. I'll deal with you later."

"Yes, sir." Dinah's wide-eyed glance swung between Caroline and her husband.

Caroline tried to reassure her with a smile, but her lips would not cooperate. A nod was all she could manage.

Luke closed the door behind Dinah, his lips tightly compressed. Eyes blazing, he looked around the room, his gaze taking in all the details of the parlor she and Dinah had made comfortable. He grunted when he noticed the newspaper they had been using for their lesson. "Are you determined to bring us all down to your level, Caroline?"

Caroline opened her mouth to tell him about how she and Dinah had become as close as sisters. Dinah wouldn't cause any trouble. Perhaps she could make him understand. "I'm sorry, Luke. I was—"

"I can see what you were doing. Do you have so little sense? Can you possibly think it is acceptable to teach a slave to read?" He stepped toward her and grasped her by the shoulders. "You've probably ruined Dinah. And if anyone else finds out she's been taught to read, I'll have to hang her. Do you want her death on your conscience?"

A vision of her friend's lifeless body hanging from the thick limb of an oak tree flashed into Caroline's mind. She could almost hear the creak of the rope and the sobs of her husband and children.

"Who knows what ideas you've put in that girl's head?" Luke's thunderous tones pulled her away from the horrible vision. "Ideas that could lead to sedition and insurrection. Can't you understand the danger of a slave uprising? You and my grandmother could be murdered in your beds. Is that what you want?"

"No." Caroline swallowed hard and twisted away from his grasp. She didn't want to hear any more. "Of course not."

She searched for a way to get through Luke's anger and calm him enough so she could explain about Dinah's wish to read from the Bible. Caroline wanted to share with him the joy of watching a new world open up for her friend, a world with endless delights and wonderful possibilities. A world all people, no matter their race, should be able to access.

"Then why did you do this? You had to know it was

wrong." His eyebrows lowered even farther. "You brought her out here in secret. You lied to my grandmother about your reason for leaving the house. Is that any way to act?"

Caroline felt the blow of his accusation as her own conscience condemned her. He was right. She had lied or at least obscured the truth. What kind of Christian was she? Her parents would be so disappointed. Tears of conviction threatened, but she was determined to hold them back. She needed to keep calm even though she wanted nothing more than to put her face in her hands and cry her eyes out. How else could she show him she was not a child?

Luke strode to the window, his rigid back to her. "Caroline, I forbid you to teach Dinah or any other slave how to read and write. And you are not to come back out here again, at least not until I return home." He turned around to her once more. The planes of his face were sharp, as hard as granite. "I don't know what to think about you, Caroline. You're not the girl I thought you were. You're as deceitful as Delilah, eager to do anything to get your own way. I seem to only be capable of falling for women who do nothing but deceive me."

Caroline shook her head. He could not be saying what she thought. He could not be telling her he was sorry he had married her. Yes, she had faults. Many of them. And she still had so much to learn about how Luke wanted her to conduct herself.

"I should have listened to Grandma's advice and married Marianna Lister. Maybe I should return to Vicksburg and apologize for not realizing sooner what a paragon she really is." He turned around and shoved his cap back onto his head. "I wish I'd never come."

The pain caused by his words was as sharp as the thrust of a sword. Her heart shattered into a million pieces. Unable to stay in the room with him another minute, she turned and ran from the parlor. Tears streamed down her cheeks.

She stuffed her fist in her mouth to keep from bawling like a frightened calf and ran down the steps. It didn't matter where she was headed. Caroline's only thought was to put some distance between them.

Branches slapped at her, but she continued running blindly until her breath came in gasps and her side screamed its pain. It wasn't until she was forced to stop that Caroline realized no matter how fast or far she ran she could not get away from his words. The words she never thought she would hear Luke say. The words no woman should have to live with. Her husband wished he had married another woman.

&

Caroline dragged herself up the front steps and fell against the door. Looking down, she realized her skirts were dirty and torn from her mad dash through the woods. Her hair was a mess, too. She put up a shaky hand to straighten it but couldn't begin to make herself presentable. Maybe she could slip up to her room without being seen. Dinah would help. . . if Dinah was still allowed to tend to her.

A sob broke past her lips. She turned the cold brass knob and slipped inside the hall she'd once thought cold and formal but now realized had become home to her. Was she about to lose the right to think of Shady Oaks as her home?

"Caroline?" Grandma Darby descended the central staircase, her dark dress swaying around her as she rushed to the first floor. "Where have you been? Where's Luke?"

A seemingly endless supply of tears filled her eyes. "I—I don't know."

"What's happened? Was there an accident? Do I need to send someone for Luke?" She gasped and put a hand over her mouth. "He's not dead, is he?"

Caroline shook her head. "We had a fight. I think he's g—gone."

Grandma Darby's eyes widened. She looked around the foyer and pointed at one of the footmen. "Go get Dinah. Send her to Miss Caroline's room with clean towels and fresh water." She put a supporting arm around Caroline's waist. "Let's get you upstairs. Then you can tell me all about it."

She felt older than the woman helping her up the stairs. As though everything good in her life was behind her, the future unfolded before her weary eyes, bleak and void of happiness. Tears flowed once more.

Grandma Darby pushed open the bedroom door with her free hand. "I don't know what's wrong, Caroline, but I know it can be fixed."

The colorful quilt atop her bed beckoned, but Caroline felt too grimy to yield. Instead she chose the straight-backed chair in front of her writing desk.

Grandma Darby dabbed her handkerchief into the bowl of water on her dresser and used it to clean Caroline's face. "You should not despair. You are a Christian. You know all things are possible for us. Jesus will see us through the hard times."

Another wave of shame engulfed Caroline. She was supposed to be a Christian. So where was her faith? A tiny glimmer of hope appeared in her mind, like a flickering candle in the vastness of the midnight sky. Her tears slowed, and she hiccupped.

A knock on the door brought her head up. "Luke?" Hope and fear mingled in her chest.

The door opened, and Dinah stepped through. "I'm so glad you're back, miss. I worried about you."

Caroline stuffed the hope back down.

Dinah put down her burdens and went to the chest holding Caroline's clothing. "We'd better get you changed."

Grandma Darby and Dinah fussed over her, brushing her hair and removing her dirty clothing. She recounted the argument she had with Luke while they helped her bathe, cleaning the painful scrapes and scratches the forest had inflicted on her.

"If it makes things any easier for you, you don't have to tell me why the two of you have been disappearing into the woods every day." Grandma Darby helped Caroline into a fresh gown. "I've seen the closeness between you, and I know about your background, Caroline—the antislavery leanings of your parents and grandparents. I suspect you've been teaching Dinah to read."

Caroline gasped. "You do?"

Grandma Darby rolled her eyes. "I may be old, but I'm not senile, young lady. I can still reason out a thing or two."

"Of course you can." Caroline leaned back against her pillows. "I'm just surprised you haven't tried to stop us."

"Perhaps I should have, but everything seems to be changing, even the basic rules governing society. I suppose I decided to look the other way because I'm simply no longer certain that I'm right."

Even though she was worried about Luke and their future, a part of Caroline marveled over the change in his grandmother. She had gone from being petty and narrow-minded to a woman who was learning to tolerate, if not embrace, new ideas. "The next thing we'll hear is that you want to set Dinah and the others free."

"Remember the day the runaway slaves appeared on our doorstep?" asked Grandma Darby.

Caroline nodded, too weary to talk.

Grandma Darby fussed with an edge of Caroline's sheet. "I listened to those men talk about their emancipation, and I realized they were as determined as my husband to make their way in the world. It came to me that perhaps they deserved that chance. I'll never forget the way you handled them either. You were wonderful."

Any other time, Caroline might have blushed at the complimentary words, but tonight she was far too weary. She watched as Grandma Darby and Dinah banked the fire in her fireplace. Then they blew out the candles and tiptoed out. She watched the dancing flames until they blurred and dimmed. Her last thought as sleep claimed her was that she had to reach Luke and convince him not to end their marriage.

fourteen

Her stomach heaved as Caroline sat up on the side of her bed. She lay back down and pulled her knees up toward her chin. It must be a reaction to all the emotional upheaval caused by Luke's unexpected arrival. How she had hoped she would wake up and discover that the scene was nothing more than a nightmare. A headache pounded between her temples, and her eyes felt raw and swollen—indications that her hope was in vain.

The door opened, and Dinah slipped inside. She filled Caroline's washbasin with fresh water and stoked the fire.

Caroline sat up and tried to summon a smile. "Good morning."

"Good morning, Miss Caroline. I hope you slept well."

"I suppose so. But I feel pretty awful this morning."

Dinah's brown eyes were sad "I'm so sorry about all of this."

The concerned tone helped Caroline focus on something besides her own misery. She swung her legs over the side of the bed. "It's not your fault. I wanted to teach you to read. But I should have approached it differently."

"How?"

Caroline stood and pulled Dinah to her for a hug. "I don't know. But you don't have to worry about it I'll make sure you don't suffer because of it." After a momentary stiffness, Dinah relaxed and hugged her back. The contact eased Caroline's grief slightly. She pulled back and wiped a tear from her cheek. "It's going to be okay. I promise you that."

"I believe you." Dinah sniffed and turned away. "Why don't we get you dressed so you can go downstairs and eat?"

Queasiness attacked her again at the thought of food, but Caroline swallowed hard against it. She had to go downstairs and begin mending the scraps of her life. She bathed her face in the warm water Dinah had brought. She chose a pale-blue dress, hoping to lift her spirits. But judging by the heaviness weighing on her shoulders as she descended the stairs, Caroline knew her plan had failed.

"There you are, my dear." Grandma Darby gave her a kind smile.

The smell of fried bacon was usually a pleasant smell to Caroline, but this morning her stomach turned over. She nodded to her grandmother-in-law and slid into her seat, turning down a plate of eggs and bacon. "Just a piece of dry toast."

Grandma Darby frowned. "You'd better eat more than that. You're going to need all your strength if we're going to put my plan into action."

Caroline's stomach shifted once more. She needed to turn Grandma Darby's attention to something else. "What plan is that?"

"I was thinking of what you told me last night. If there's one thing I learned in my years of living with Luke's grandfather, it's that a married couple should never let an argument fester. The longer you allow differences to separate you, the harder it will be to bridge the gap. You and Luke have an additional challenge since you are physically separated by his army duty."

Caroline looked at Luke's grandmother with new eyes. The woman had surprised her last night when she'd been so kind and supportive. Now she was talking about the weaknesses in her own marriage. Making herself more vulnerable than Caroline would have ever dreamed possible.

"He was so angry—" Her voice broke on the last word. Clenching her hands, she took a deep breath. "I—I don't know when he'll come home."

Grandma Darby dabbed at her mouth with one of the linen napkins. "That's why we need to go to him."

Go to Vicksburg? Caroline's tears dried up. "But we can't travel alone."

"Humbug." Grandma Darby threw her napkin on the table with force, raising her eyebrows in a defiant gesture. "Why not?"

Where should she begin? The dangers of traveling were always high, especially for two women without a male escort. But now those dangers had multiplied. What if they had met the group of fleeing slaves while on their journey? She shuddered. "I can think of many reasons we should not attempt such a journey."

"Start with the first few."

Caroline took a deep breath. "Deserters, escaping slaves, renegade Yankees, and we could find ourselves in the middle of a battle."

"I see." Grandma Darby's put her hands on the table and pushed herself up. "I'm starting to believe you don't think your marriage is worth the risk."

"That's not true."

The look Luke's grandmother tossed at her was a challenge. "I can be packed in an hour. How long will it take you?"

Caroline took a bite out of her toast. Madness. Could they even make it to Vicksburg before nightfall?

Grandma Darby exited the dining room as Caroline considered the possibility. The idea tempted her. But what would Luke say when they arrived? Would he listen to her after letting a few hours pass? Or would he still cling to his anger?

An even worse possibility crept into her mind: *what if he*

had turned to Marianna Lister for comfort? What if he was even now telling the avid young woman all about their argument? What if he was kissing—

She broke off the thought before it could take root in her mind. She didn't need to torture herself with implausible scenarios. Luke was an honorable man. He would never break his marriage vows. But like an insidious weed, the image popped back into her head. Caroline pushed her plate away and stood up. Perhaps she could eradicate it by concentrating on readying herself for the trip.

At least her stomach had settled after her breakfast. She moved slowly up the stairs to her bedroom and pulled the cord to summon Dinah. She would have to remember to ask for fresh bread. Otherwise it would be an uncomfortable trip for all of them.

❧

"I still don't quite see why we had to come back to Vicksburg in such an almighty hurry." Hezekiah's face wore a confused frown. "I thought we was going to stay at Shady Oaks overnight."

"I changed my mind. A good thing, too, since I received orders this morning to report to the main headquarters."

Even though the sun was shining down on them, a fog seemed to surround Luke. Was he wrong? Should he have been more gentle with Caroline? He hadn't meant to make her run from him. But he had a duty to stop her from making foolish mistakes. A good husband protected his wife, even if it was from her own self.

What about Marianna Lister? The accusing words made him cringe inside. Well, he was man enough to admit he should not have said anything about Miss Lister.

Luke knew he had lost control. It was one of the reasons he had decided to leave immediately after confronting his wife. He'd been angry, and he had lashed out at her in the harshest way possible, determined to make her as unhappy as he was. Her devastated expression haunted him, but he could do little about it. Perhaps he would pen a note of apology to her this evening. If General Pemberton agreed, he might even be able to take off a few days next week and spend them with her and Grandma.

They entered the main headquarters, Hezekiah falling two paces behind. After looking around for a minute, Luke spotted a group of men studying a large map that had been nailed to the wall. He joined them and listened to the discussion.

"Our cannons will keep the city safe from a river assault." The man speaking was General Pemberton. He nodded to Luke but continued talking to the officers around him. "And we're well fortified here, here, and here." He pointed to several spots north, south, and east of the city. "But those are only a precaution. The Union has never been able to get a toehold on this side of the river, thanks to men like Captain Talbot here."

Caught off guard by the use of his name, Luke saluted. "It hasn't been without cost, sir."

"Yes, that's true." Pemberton turned his attention back to the map. "We all hope and pray the lives lost will not be in vain." He continued outlining the defense preparations of Vicksburg, patiently answering questions and listening to suggestions.

"Our spies tell us Grant is on the march." Pemberton pointed to the far side of the Mississippi River, tracing an inland route to the south. "But he has no way to get his troops across the river because his boats are all bottled up to our north. Unless he has a way to spirit them past my cannons, he will fail to get the support he needs to launch another attack against Vicksburg."

"Perhaps he plans to march to New Orleans." The suggestion came from one of the officers standing next to Luke.

Pemberton frowned. "It is possible, but unlikely. Some of you were here when two boats sailed past our cannons in the middle of the night. I think it is more likely he will try to accomplish a second nighttime run with more of his ships. So we need men over in Louisiana who can set signal fires to backlight any boats that try to get past us." He looked at Luke. "I want you to take a few men across the river. Your mission will be to set up bonfires that can be lit at a moment's notice. As soon as the boats are in sight, you'll have to set the signal fires and sneak back across the river to avoid being targets yourselves."

Luke's chest expanded. He saluted. "Yes, sir." Pemberton would only assign such a mission to someone he trusted. The shadow of his actions in Knoxville had finally lifted. He was accepted as a valuable member of the Confederate army.

If only Caroline would value him as others did. . .

fifteen

"Wake up, Caroline." A gentle hand shook her shoulder. "We're in Vicksburg."

Caroline opened her eyes to see Grandma Darby smiling. She sat up and looked out the carriage window, surprised to see that dusk had fallen. "I must have fallen asleep."

"I imagine you didn't sleep very well last night. But now that we are going to face the problem headfirst, you were able to relax and catch up on what you missed."

She hoped Grandma Darby's analysis was correct. It was true she'd felt very foggy this morning, but her mind didn't feel much clearer even after her hours-long nap. The very thought of facing Luke's anger once again made her stomach clench. Could she do it?

The nausea she'd felt back at Shady Oaks returned with suddenness. Choking it down, she watched the older lady gather her things. Something in her behavior seemed odd, as though Grandma Darby was nervous. "What's wrong?"

"I—I don't know how to broach the subject of our accommodations with you."

Dread flitted into her disgruntled stomach, its dark wings spreading fear. In all the months she'd observed Luke's grandmother, she had never heard her stutter. What could be that wrong?

"All of the hotels in town are filled to overflowing. There's no room for us at all tonight."

This was bad news indeed. "What are we going to do?"

"I've sent some of our slaves to make inquiries, but we will have to stay with friends this evening. Unfortunately, many of my friends have fled the city because of the rumors of an impending attack." Grandma Darby stopped talking and pulled at a loose thread on her glove. "Fortunately, I have discovered one family who is still here and has opened their home to us."

"Who?" The single word hung in the thick air of the carriage. Caroline put a hand to her chest in an attempt to quell her heart's flutter.

"Timothy and Georgia Lister. Now before. . ."

Caroline's heart stopped. She could feel her blood congealing, and she missed something Grandma Darby said. With a thump, her heart started again, and she sucked in a deep breath.

"I know this is the last place you want to spend a night, but it simply cannot be helped." Grandma Darby grimaced. "If you are the woman I think you are, you will overcome this hurdle. And tomorrow, as soon as a place has been found, we will take our leave. And we can send a message to Luke at headquarters. He'll likely come right over, and the two of you can reconcile."

Caroline could imagine the scene. Luke would sit on one end of the couch, and she would sit on the other. Marianna would either sit inside the parlor with them or lean against the door so she could hear every word. She shook her head. "Maybe I should visit Luke instead."

If she had not been so heartsick, Caroline would have laughed at the shock on Grandma Darby's face. "At the garrison? That would never do. Your reputation would be irredeemable."

A sigh of resignation filled her as she watched Grandma Darby alight from the coach. She sent up a prayer for strength to survive the evening before following her husband's relative, the one who had once advised him to not marry her.

The front of the Lister house was formidable. It stood three stories high and spread outward from the central entrance like a European castle. If she had not lived for the past months at an even larger, more imposing home, Caroline would have turned and run in the opposite direction. But she had spent time at Shady Oaks, so she lifted her skirts and entered the Lister home with her head held high.

≥∾

Vicksburg's high bluffs cast deep shadows, and the sky overhead seemed to pull a black cloak over its expanse. The river drifted away to the south, unconcerned with the battles being fought along its length.

Sweat trickled into Luke's eyes as he pushed hard on the pole and silently moved his pirogue, the flat-bottomed boat popular on both sides of the Mississippi, through the swampy reeds lining the riverbank. They were patrolling the water as ordered, looking for any sign the Yankees had decided to test the Confederate cannons tonight.

"Watch that branch." Hezekiah whispered a warning.

Luke ducked and felt the pointed needles of a cypress tree brush the back of his head. "Thanks, that was close." He glanced back at his companion, noticing how Hezekiah's hands clung to both sides of the boat. "Are you worried the river is going to reach up and drag you in?"

Hezekiah's eyes widened. "Don't you tease me, Master Luke. You know how scared I am of the water. I don't want to fall in and drown."

"It'll be okay. We won't be getting out of the boat unless we have to light the signal fires."

Water lapped against the side of the boat, rocking it slightly. Luke strained his eyes, looking for what had caused the wavelets. "Look, what is that?"

"I can't see. . .No, wait. I see it. Something's out there, but I can't tell exactly what it is. It don't look much like a boat to me."

"It must be the Yankees."

"What do we do now?" The fear in Hezekiah's voice was much clearer than the outline of the boat trying to slip past.

"We've got to get to the other side of the river and get those signals lit."

"But we can't go now. Not with all them Yankees just waiting to shoot us out of the water. We'll get run down for sure."

"This would be a good time for you to pray," suggested Luke. He took a moment to send his own request toward heaven, just in case God was listening.

With a grunt, he pushed away from the bank. Earlier he and Hezekiah had wrapped their oars in cloth to muffle the sound they made. Now they dipped the oars slowly to further disguise any telltale noise.

The river rushed around them, trying to push their little boat south toward the Gulf of Mexico. Darkness provided cover for the pirogue as it made slow but steady progress across to the Louisiana side of the river. No moon brightened the sky, a fact that had no doubt influenced the Yankees to choose tonight to move their fleet.

Luke and Hezekiah made it across without incident and landed on the little beach Luke had scouted earlier in the day. "I guess your prayers worked," Luke whispered as they stowed the pirogue. "I sure am glad you and God are so close."

Hezekiah nodded and smiled, his teeth white against the dark skin of his face.

The two men made their way silently along the soft bank until they reached the first pile of firewood and dry brush.

Luke withdrew a lucifer from his pocket and started the blaze before moving to the next pile of wood. Five piles, five fires. The two men stood back and watched as the blackness was penetrated by the blazes, providing a backdrop to highlight the positions of the ships on the water. Almost immediately, cannons on the opposite shore began their bombardment.

Luke wiped his grimy hands on his pants. "Let's get back to the pirogue. We're easy targets ourselves as long as we stand in front of this fire."

"Will we be safe down there?"

"I would think so. The Yanks aren't going to be interested in this side of the river. Those cannons will probably sink a great many of them. And the ones that are left will be concentrating their attention on the east shore. I imagine General Grant will think twice before he sends his boats this far south again. He'll probably move them back to Memphis and try to figure out what to do next."

"He's gonna be mighty surprised when his boats don't show up."

Luke nodded. "If we can keep him on this side of the river until General Johnson's troops get here to reinforce Vicksburg, I think everything will be okay. This has to work. We have to keep control of Vicksburg. If we lose Vicksburg, we lose the whole river and probably the war."

The two men returned to the riverbank, not bothering to hide their progress this time because of the uproar on the water. The Yanks were returning fire, but their bullets could not reach the Confederate cannons located on the high bluffs on the eastern side of the river. And they were taking a pounding because the Confederate soldiers could see them so clearly against the fiery sky. Luke could hear the explosions as cannonballs struck the decks of the ironclads.

As they reached their boat, he winced at the cries of wounded and dying soldiers. He climbed into the front of the boat and turned to face Hezekiah. "There's a creek I noticed just south of here when we came over this afternoon. Do you remember it?"

The slave shook his head. "I wasn't looking at much except all that water underneath us."

Luke allowed his mouth to relax into a smile. "You really are frightened of the water, aren't you?"

A nod answered him.

"The creek you missed looked like it might offer some protection. Maybe we can even find a cave to keep us safe until the morning. There's not much we can do from here, and I don't have the stomach for shooting any of the men who make it to the shore."

"Me neither, Master Luke. That seems like something the good Lord would frown on."

"I agree." Luke untied the rope tethering their boat to the shore and stood up to push them out into the channel. An odd sound, not unlike the buzz of a hornet, filled his ears. An instant later he felt a fire light in his leg.

"Master Luke!"

He heard the scream as if from a distance. Then the oddest thing happened. The river rose up and slapped him in the face. For an instant, the cold water brought him back to clarity. *I've been shot.* He tried to swim to safety, but the powerful currents dragged him away from the bank. As the inky waters closed over his head, Luke heard an ominous splash behind him. He wondered if being eaten by an alligator would be a more unpleasant way to die than drowning.

sixteen

Caroline tossed her quilt back and rose from the unfamiliar bed. What had awakened her? The question was answered as the sky outside her bedroom window lit up. A firefight was being waged somewhere nearby. Her hand went to her throat as another volley of cannon fire boomed. Was the city being attacked?

She pulled back the curtains. The street behind the Lister home was quiet, but some distance away she could see people out on the street, carrying torches. Were they Yankee soldiers? Had the city fallen? Caroline closed her eyes and prayed for safety for those in the Lister home, for the soldiers fighting on both sides, and especially for her husband.

Noises in the hallway indicated she was not the only one who had been awakened by the commotion outside. Grabbing her wrapper and pulling it on, Caroline opened the door.

"There's no need to be scared." Marianna was speaking to her younger siblings. The candle she held cast a glow on her face. She looked beautiful even when pulled from her bed in the middle of the night. Combined with her jet-black hair and large eyes, her image put Caroline in mind of paintings of the Madonna.

Marianna's parents appeared at the same time as Grandma Darby, each having the presence of mind to light a candle.

"All of you women stay up here while I go see what is going on." Mr. Lister's dark brows were drawn together in a frown. He had taken time to pull on a pair of trousers, but his nightshirt still hung down to his knees.

Another volley of cannon fire made the younger girls scream and run to their mother. Marianna ran to the balustrade and looked over.

Caroline would have joined her to see what was going on downstairs, but Grandma Darby was looking quite shaken so she walked to her instead. "Are you okay?" Her worried gaze searched the older woman's face.

Grandma Darby's smile was wobbly on her face, but she straightened her shoulders and nodded. Gray hair peeked out from the edges of her crocheted nightcap. "I am worried about Luke."

"I know. I've been praying for him since I woke up."

More cannon fire brought all of the females to the edge of the balustrade. The front door stood open, allowing them to glimpse the street outside.

Caroline reached for Grandma Darby's hand. "It sounds like it is coming from the river."

"That would make sense." Marianna looked toward her. "But I wonder if the Yankees are really foolish enough to attack us from the water. They should know by now they will never succeed with that."

Mrs. Lister nodded her agreement with her oldest daughter's statement. "Our bluffs are high enough to hold off any attackers."

Footsteps on the stairs drew their attention to the return of Mr. Lister. His face was calm, relaxed. Seeing his expression made Caroline feel better.

"Don't worry, ladies. There's no cause for alarm. The cannons you hear are ours. A flotilla of Yankee ships are trying to use the darkness to float past us, but we're ready for them." He turned and pointed toward the front door. "See that red glow in the distance?"

Caroline looked to the area where he pointed. An eerie radiance pierced the darkness almost like seeing the sun rise. But unless she was mistaken, she was looking west.

"We've got dozens of signal fires lit on the Louisiana side of the river to backlight the Yankees. Makes their boats clear targets. Our cannons are most likely sending all of them to the bottom of the river."

"You see, girls," Mrs. Lister spoke gently to her younger children, "we have nothing to fear. I would suggest all of us return to our rooms and try to sleep." She herded the children to the nursery.

Marianna talked to her father about what he had seen and heard.

Caroline wanted to listen to the man's answers but knew she needed to support Grandma Darby. Putting an arm around her waist, she walked back toward the other woman's bedroom. "I think Mrs. Lister is right."

"I should not have insisted we come to Vicksburg." Grandma Darby blew out her candle and placed it on the table beside her bed. "It has put both of us in harm's way, and it seems unlikely you'll get to talk to Luke with all of this going on."

Caroline's heart went out to Luke's grandmother. She sounded so weary, so lost. "Don't worry about it. You couldn't know the Union soldiers were about to launch their ships. And you were trying to help me get things sorted out." She stood next to Grandma Darby's bed. "Why don't we say a prayer for Luke's safety before I leave you?"

Grandma Darby nodded. "That's a wonderful idea."

They knelt side by side. Caroline steepled her hands and closed her eyes. "Lord, we come to You with frightened hearts tonight. Please protect Luke. Keep him safe from harm. Please don't let his anger remain. And help me find a way to mend the breach between us." She fell silent as God's Spirit seemed to settle around her. What a wonderful Maker she served. Even in the midst of danger and fear, He was faithful to listen to her and answer her pleas.

Grandma Darby shifted. "Lord, You heal the lame and give sight to the blind. Please watch over my grandson. Wrap him in Your loving arms. Give him strength and cunning. He's not bulletproof, Lord, so please cover him with Your protection. Thank You, Lord. We pray in the precious name of Your Son who died for us. Amen."

Caroline pushed herself up and helped Grandma Darby into bed. After pulling the quilt up, she leaned over and gave the woman's wrinkled cheek a swift kiss. "Sleep well."

"You, too, dearest Caroline."

The words echoed in her head as she made her way slowly back to her bedroom. She was almost too tired to put one foot in front of the other. Now that she knew they were not in immediate danger, she felt like wrung-out laundry, not even removing her wrapper as she crawled back into her bed.

After a little while, she realized the cannon fire had stopped. The battle was over. So why did she feel so uneasy?

A compulsion overcame her to pray. Obedient even though she didn't understand, Caroline got out of the bed once more and sank to her knees. She started by praying once again for her husband's safety, but the words somehow got twisted and lost. Supplication filled her, containing all her pleas, hopes, and dreams for a future with the man she loved.

Time ceased to exist as the prayer continued. Finally, when it was over, she stood once more, surprised to look out the window and see that dawn was quickly approaching. Even though she knew God had heard her prayers, she couldn't completely quiet the whisper of dread trying to envelop her heart.

When Dinah entered her room with a tray, Caroline woke to realize the sun was high in the sky. "Why did you let me sleep for so long?"

"You needed the rest."

"That's what Grandma Darby said yesterday. It seems all I do is sleep these days." Caroline sat up in bed and chose a piece of toast from the tray

"It's only natural since you're in the family way."

Caroline gasped as though doused with a bucket of icy water. "What do you mean?"

"Now, Miss Caroline, you had to notice your dresses have been getting tighter. And then you been getting sick in the early morning. It's only natural after all."

Her face flamed, and Caroline didn't know where to look. She was going to have a baby! How she wished she could tell Ma and Pa the good news. They would be so excited. If not for this beastly war, she could plan a trip to visit with them or at least send them a letter to tell them the good news, but for now she would have to celebrate with her new family. She and Luke were going to be parents. What would he say? How could she even tell him?

She finished the toasted bread and got up so Dinah could help her get dressed in one of the gowns that had indeed seemed to shrink over the past weeks. She had thought it was because of the rich food offered at Shady Oaks. "How long have you known?"

"Nearly a month." Dinah straightened Caroline's skirt with quick motions and stepped back. "But I doubt anybody else knows, exceptin' maybe Missus Darby. You got time to tell Master Luke, but you better do it quick. Now go on while I clean up your room. They're waiting for you in the parlor."

Was Luke here? Her heart beat faster. *Thank You, God.*

Had a day ever held such promise?

Caroline practically flew down the steps. Forgetting proper decorum, she burst through the parlor door to find the room full. Grandma Darby, Mr. and Mrs. Lister, Marianna, and a swarthy man she did not recognize. But where was Luke? Her footsteps faltered. Why was Grandma Darby dabbing her face with a handkerchief? Why were the rest of the people in the room looking at her with such sadness?

Caroline wanted to turn and run back upstairs. She needed to get back into her bed. Maybe sleep awhile longer. Anything to postpone this meeting.

She didn't want to step inside the room, but before Caroline could turn away, Marianna jumped up and ran to her. "Oh, my dear, I am so sorry."

Tears pushed at her eyes. "What is it? What's happened?"

The swarthy man had stood at her entrance, and now he bowed to her. "Mrs. Talbot, allow me to introduce myself. I am Major Michel Fontenot."

"Michel—I mean, Major Fontenot—is a friend of the family." Marianna had a death grip on her arm. "He is also Luke's commanding officer." She hesitated for a moment, swallowing hard. "I'm afraid he has some bad news."

Caroline would have covered her ears if not for Marianna's grasp. She knew she didn't want to hear whatever it was this man had to say. It was the news that was making Grandma Darby weep. It would make her weep, too. "No."

Fontenot's dark gaze was sad as he nodded. "Your husband and his slave took part in a very risky venture last night, one that gave us a distinct advantage. They crossed the river and lit signal fires to unveil the ships trying to defeat Vicksburg's defenses. Their actions may have kept the city safe, but sadly, they paid the ultimate price."

"No." It seemed the only word she could say.

Marianna drew her to the sofa. "I am so sorry."

Caroline looked up at her and saw the sympathy in the other woman's gaze. The smell of wood smoke from the fireplace threatened to choke her. The air in the room seemed dense with it.

As if from a distance she could hear the others talking. They were saying things about bravery and courage, concepts that had no meaning in this moment. She coughed and took the handkerchief someone handed her, not knowing whether she was about to cry or lose the contents of her stomach. . . .

Another realization dawned—she was carrying Luke's child. And now she would never be able to share her joy with him. Her dreams of a happy future disappeared in an instant, replaced by grief and despair. How could this have happened? Why did God allow it to happen? How would she ever recover?

seventeen

Intense thirst pulled Luke to consciousness. He looked around and realized he was in a cave. The crackling flames from a nearby fire held the damp night air at bay. Every part of his body was racked with pain, but he was relieved to find himself still alive.

A shuffling noise brought his head around to see Hezekiah entering the cave with a skinned rabbit in one hand. "Master Luke? It's good to see you awake."

Luke tried to push himself up, but a shooting pain made his eyes water. The walls of the cave swam dizzily.

"Don't you try to sit up yet, Master Luke. You been shot." Hezekiah draped the rabbit over a nearby rock and helped Luke lie back down.

That must be why he ached so. Luke caught his breath after a few seconds. "What happened? How long have we been here?"

Hezekiah squatted next to him and stirred at the fire. "We been here 'bout a week now, and you been pretty sick."

"What happened?" Luke repeated his first question. "All I remember is coming across the river to light signal fires."

"That's right, Master Luke. And we got those fires all lit up. It'll be a wonder if any of them boats made it past our cannons. You and I was about to hole up until morning, but someone musta' seen us. They started firing, and since you was at the front of the boat, you took a bullet right here." Hezekiah's finger lightly grazed a spot above Luke's knee.

The area he touched was very tender, but that was not

what made Luke start. "I remember! I fell into the water, and a gator splashed in after me. I thought I was dead for sure."

Hezekiah's chuckle was deep and rich. "That wasn't no gator. That was me you heard."

"Were you hit, too, then?"

"No."

Luke wished he could sit up, but he was too weak. "You jumped in the water after me?"

Hezekiah nodded and busied himself with readying a spit for their meal.

"But you're afraid of the water. You can't even swim. Why would you do such a thing?"

"You told me you got doubts about what you believe—so I knew if you died, your soul would belong to Satan, and he'd torment you for all eternity."

Luke's breath stopped. He could feel his heart thudding in his chest. He didn't know what to say. He'd never realized the depth of the slave's faith. "You risked your life to save me."

Hezekiah shrugged. "You're my neighbor. Jesus says we have to love God first and each other next. I couldn't let you die."

The words were simple but so strong. Warmth spread throughout his body, warmth that had nothing to do with the flames of the nearby fire. It was the whisper of God reaching out to him through Hezekiah's faith and willingness to sacrifice his own life. He was humbled. Tears stung his eyes. Gone was all his arrogance, his belief that God was too distant to care about him. "I want to know this Savior."

"Praise the Lord. He wants to know you, too." A smile relaxed Hezekiah's face. "There must be a big celebration going on in heaven right now. Another sheep is coming to the Father."

Hezekiah talked about his own walk with Christ. His

words seemed to flow directly into Luke's soul.

Luke's heart had been a hardened, dry sponge. Now it swelled and softened as the love of Jesus entered. In the flickering light inside the cave, he gave his life to Christ. The Holy Spirit took up residence inside him, and the terrible anguish began to ease.

A spiritual hunger awakened inside him. He wanted to know more. He wanted to follow Christ. "I've been such an idiot. Would you pray with me? I don't know what to say to Jesus."

Hezekiah nodded. "I remember the first time I talked to Him out loud. It was a scary thing. Like you finally realize how big and powerful He is, and you wonder how you can dare to speak to Him."

"Yes, you do understand. When I look back at the things I've done, I wonder how God can forgive me."

"It's a mighty strong God who loves you, Luke. He's ready to forgive you. All you have to do is ask Him to come inside you."

Tears fell from his closed eyes as Luke prayed for Christ to enter his heart. He went from feeling dirty and unworthy to feeling the wonder of a Savior who loved him and who gave His blood to wash away Luke's sins. Faith was more than attending church or reading a Bible. It was a personal relationship with his Maker. When the prayer was finished, Luke knew the rest of his life was going to be different. He had made a lot of mistakes, but Christ did not condemn him.

His mind went to his wife. *Caroline.* As if a veil had been lifted, he realized she was the only woman he had ever really loved. He had fallen once for a beautiful girl back home and had even tried to correct that mistake by courting Marianna Lister, a girl for whom he had no tender feelings. But he thanked God for leading him to Caroline instead.

His heart cracked as he thought of the harsh words he'd thrown at her the last time they had been together. How had she fared after he deserted her? Would she forgive him as quickly as Christ had? He didn't know the answer to the questions, but he did know one thing. If it took him the rest of his life, he would seek her forgiveness and treat her with the love and respect she deserved.

He would return to Vicksburg only long enough to resign his position. Then he would find his wife at Shady Oaks, and with God's help, he would make things right between them.

That is, if Caroline would allow him to. . .

❧

The fever came back the next day. Luke tried not to thrash about, but the fire inside his body made him restless. From time to time, Hezekiah gave him cool water or placed a wet cloth on his face. The relief did not last.

The next time Luke's mind cleared, they were on the move. Hezekiah must have built a travois. It was not an easy ride, but it had to be much harder on his slave to pull the framework holding Luke.

"Hezekiah." His throat was so parched he could barely croak, but the man carrying him heard the sound.

"Yes, Master Luke?" He carefully lowered the travois and offered Luke water from a canteen. "You feeling a little better?"

"You're a miracle, Hezekiah." He coughed.

Hezekiah shook his head. "I'm just a man."

"From this day forward, consider yourself a free man. I can't ever repay the debt I owe you."

"You don't owe me nothing."

"I owe you my life, twice over now."

"That's not why I saved you, Master Luke."

"I know that. You were prompted by a higher desire. You

are a true child of God." He reached for the canteen and took another mouthful of water before continuing. "You're also my brother in Christ. Even if I don't make it, you tell Caroline I said to free all of the slaves."

Hezekiah stood and lifted the travois once more. "Don't you go talking like that, Master Luke. I'll get you back to a doctor, and he'll fix you up right quick-like."

Luke barely heard Hezekiah begin to plead with God for Luke's life as he faded from consciousness again.

eighteen

"It's time to consider going back home." Grandma Darby returned her teacup to the silver service on the table at her elbow. "This hotel is nice, but it's not home. And with all the Yankees in Mississippi right now, I'm worried we'll get back to Shady Oaks to find nothing but a pile of ashes."

Caroline punched her needle downward through the pillowcase. "I'm not giving up on Luke." She had designed a stylized T entwined in oak leaves to decorate the linens, but now the green threads blurred into unrecognizable shapes as tears gathered in her eyes. Her sore nose burned—not surprising since she had spent a large portion of the past week crying. But she clung to the belief that her husband and Hezekiah were still alive. She couldn't explain it to Grandma Darby, or anyone else for that matter, because her hope. . .her belief. . .was not based on any solid evidence. She might be leaning on a spider web, but for now it was the only way she could get through each day.

A feminine scream from somewhere inside the hotel interrupted her thoughts. "Who was that?" Caroline sprang from her chair and rushed to open the parlor door.

Grandma Darby was slower but reached the top of the stairwell not many seconds after Caroline. "It sounds like it's coming from the front entrance."

A small group of people, mostly the hotel workers judging by their aprons and caps, had gathered near the doorway. Someone was lying on the floor. It looked like Dinah. Had she been attacked?

147

Caroline hurried down the steps, her gaze focused on Dinah's prostrate form. A grizzled black man bent over her, waving his hat above her face. "What happened to Dinah?"

The black man looked up at her, and Caroline's breath caught. "Hezekiah?"

"Yes, ma'am." He stopped fanning his wife and smiled up at Caroline.

One word trembled on her lips. "Luke?" She prayed for the strength to endure whatever answer he gave her.

"He's alive, Miss Caroline, but he's mighty sick."

"Thank You, God." Relief spread through her. "Where is he?"

"I took him to the hospital."

Caroline was already halfway back up the staircase when Dinah recovered from her swoon. She could hear her slave's happy exclamations as she reassured Grandma Darby. They hugged each other, their grateful tears mingling.

Grandma Darby finally pulled away. "Can we visit the hospital at this hour?"

Mopping her face with a sodden handkerchief, Caroline laughed. "No army in the world could keep me out."

❧

The smell of death was strong inside Anchuca, the mansion being used to shelter the wounded. Caroline's heart ached for the rows of groaning men as she followed Hezekiah. Here and there, blood-spattered doctors leaned over their patients, performing rough surgeries in the most daunting of circumstances.

"He's in here." Hezekiah walked through the wide entrance to what had once been a ballroom. Every cot was occupied, as well as most of the oak floor. A breeze slipped through the open windows and doors, cooling the room somewhat.

She barely recognized her husband as the gaunt, bearded

man lying in the cot Hezekiah stopped at. Her heart clenched. What she could see of his face looked far too pale in the light of the candles. One of his legs was bandaged, and the tattered remnants of his uniform hung in rags on him. She was shocked to see him brought so low. Where was the healthy, confident man she'd married? Was he still inside somewhere? Then his gaze landed on her face, and her heart filled to overflowing with love. Heedless of the people around her, Caroline sank to her knees and reached for his hand. "Luke. Oh, Luke, my dearest husband. Thank God you're alive."

His expression softened in wonder. "Caroline. Is it really you?"

"Yes, my darling. It's me." She pressed a kiss on the back of his hand. "I'm so glad to see you. We had reports you were dead."

He coughed weakly. "If not for Hezekiah, I would be."

"He told us what happened on the way here. It's nothing short of a miracle."

He nodded. "I have so many things to say." He coughed again.

"Not tonight, dearest. Tonight you must reserve your strength." She raised his hand to her cheek. "Tomorrow will be soon enough."

One of the doctors approached them. "Excuse me, but you'll have to leave, miss. He's very weak and needs plenty of rest." Without another word, he turned on his heel and left the room.

Caroline turned her attention to Luke. She patted his shoulder. "I'll be back tomorrow to check on you again. Please try to get plenty of rest as the doctor ordered."

Luke shook his head and motioned her to lean closer. "Take me home." His gaze, dark as midnight and desperate with need, pierced her heart.

Caroline nodded. She had no idea how they would manage, but she would honor her husband's request.

nineteen

Caroline sat in the very back of the wagon next to the pallet holding her husband. "I wonder why so many people are out after dark."

Grandma Darby was seated up front between Hezekiah and Dinah, but she must have heard Caroline's remark. "They are coming in for protection from Yankee soldiers."

Dinah nodded her agreement. "They're saying the Yanks killed thousands of soldiers the night before last."

Caroline had heard the same reports. Champion Hill had been a terrible defeat for the Confederacy. The Union army seemed unstoppable now that they had managed to get across the Mississippi River. They had taken Jackson, the state capitol, a few days earlier and were now reportedly marching ever closer to Vicksburg, gaining momentum with each successful battle. It seemed only a matter of time before the city would be taken.

Caroline noted that once they passed the outskirts of the city, the night closed in around them. "Can you see all right, Hezekiah?"

"Yes, ma'am. But I'm gonna slow down a mite."

The wagon bumped through a series of holes and ruts, causing water to slosh around in the bucket on her far side.

Luke made a sound between a groan and a grunt.

Caroline leaned over him and placed a hand on his brow. "It's all right, darling. I'm right here beside you."

"Where am I?"

"In a wagon on the way back to Shady Oaks. Grandma

151

Darby, Hezekiah, and Dinah are up front, so don't worry. We're going to take very good care of you."

She could scarcely make out his smile, but seeing it renewed her hope she was doing the right thing. It had been the hardest decision of her life, one she knew she would question many times in the days ahead. Would Luke have been better off staying in the hospital? Or would the miasma in that building have carried him off? She put a hand over the bandage on his leg, relieved that it did not feel hot. If only they could cure the infection in his chest. She hated to hear his racking cough. Caroline prayed it stemmed from something easier to combat than consumption.

A gun was fired somewhere not very far away. She felt the wagon grind to a halt as Hezekiah pulled up on the reins. She held her breath and stretched her hearing to its limits. Was someone coming toward them? No torches gleamed through the woods or from the road ahead of them. Finally Hezekiah set the horse in motion once more.

Caroline breathed a sigh of relief and dipped one of the rags she'd brought into the bucket of water before wringing it out and placing it on Luke's forehead. She continued to pray silently as they moved through the night, beseeching God to spare her husband's life and cast His protection over them on their perilous journey. The words of Psalm 23 floated through her mind, bringing her a measure of peace that lasted for nearly an hour.

"Miss Caroline, are you awake?" Hezekiah's whisper pierced the fog that had closed around her.

She shook her head to clear it. "What's wrong?"

"I think we're about to have some company."

Caroline's heart clenched as she heard the thunder of approaching hooves. Her frightened gaze met that of Luke's grandmother. Then another sound claimed her attention.

Luke's breathing had grown labored. Was he about to succumb to his illness? David's words seemed to haunt her now. *"Yea, though I walk through the valley of the shadow of death. . ."* Could she be as strong as the psalmist? Could she hold her head high and push away the fear that threatened to consume her?

Then the horses were upon them, rearing up at the last minute as their riders saw the wagon. For a few moments, everything was confusion. Hezekiah fought to keep their horse under control while the wagon rocked. By the time he had quieted the frightened animal, they were surrounded by soldiers—Yankee soldiers.

A tall man who was apparently the commanding officer pointed a gun at Hezekiah. "Who are you? Where are you going?" His voice was clipped and had an odd tone. He was obviously not from the South.

Hezekiah raised his hands to show he had no weapon. "My name is Hezekiah. I'm trying to get my master and his family back home."

"Don't you know there's a war going on?" Some of the men snickered at the leader's question.

"Of course we know that." Caroline swallowed her fear and stood. Several pistols were immediately pointed in her direction, but she ignored them, raising her chin and giving the officer her coldest stare. "But what we didn't know was that President Lincoln's army would stoop to terrorizing women."

That stopped the sly laughter, but it raised the tension in the air.

Now that her eyes had grown accustomed to the gloom of the moonless night, Caroline saw that the horsemen numbered half a dozen, so she assumed they must be advance scouts. "Our journey may seem peculiar to you, but as

Hezekiah told you, my husband is very ill. He has expressed a desire to return home, and we're doing our best to get him there. We are no threat to you and ask that you leave us in peace."

She ignored Dinah's gasp of dismay. This was no time to be timid.

The leader brought his horse toward the back of the wagon. "Where is this sick husband of yours?"

Caroline pointed downward. "Right here next to me."

The man brought his animal closer to peer at the floor of the wagon.

"What do you say, Captain?" one of the other men called to him. "Is he the spy we're trying to catch up with?"

"I will fear no evil. . ."

After a moment, the man pulled his horse away. "Nah. He's about half dead from the look of it. Besides, I don't see an extra horse. He's not our quarry."

"For thou art with me. . ." Caroline clung to the promise with all her being as she waited for the soldier to decide whether or not to detain them. *"Thy rod and thy staff they comfort me."*

"Let them pass." The man holstered his pistol and saluted her briefly. "We don't make war on women or the wounded."

"Thank you, Captain."

Hezekiah called to the horse and slapped the reins.

Caroline sat down quickly and watched as the small band of soldiers continued on their quest. *Thank You, God.*

twenty

Grandma Darby entered the bedchamber with a steaming pot balanced on a serving tray. "I think this mint infusion may bring down Luke's fever."

Caroline looked up at her from the rocking chair she had placed next to Luke's bed. Grandma Darby was looking rather frail. The ride home last night had been difficult for all of them. "Thank you."

"How is he?"

"Sometimes lucid, sometimes out of his head." Caroline bathed his face with a cool cloth. "Do you know who Amelia is?"

"No." The older woman put her burden down on the table next to the bed. "Why?"

Caroline sighed. "He's called her name twice this morning. She must be important to him."

"He's never mentioned anyone by that name to me." She paused, and comprehension entered her eyes. "He did tell me one time that he'd given his heart to a young woman in Tennessee who had deceived him. Perhaps that's who he's thinking of."

The afternoon Luke had caught her teaching Dinah to read came back with sudden intensity. He had said something then about deceitful women and his first love. At the time she'd thought he meant Marianna, but he must have meant another girl—a girl who still held his heart in her hands—a girl named Amelia.

Despair blanketed Caroline's heart at the realization. Luke

155

would never love her the way she loved him. She couldn't hurt more if she'd been struck a mortal blow. But through the pain, she felt a movement inside her. The baby!

Caroline's chin lifted. She had one thing this Amelia did not: Luke's family name. And she was carrying Luke's baby. It might not be the marriage she had once dreamed of, but Luke was her husband for better or worse. She would look for blessings in every day they spent together.

"Are you all right, Caroline?" Grandma Darby sounded concerned.

She cleared her throat and summoned a smile. "Yes, I was just thinking."

The older woman pulled a straight-backed chair beside her and took Caroline's hand in her own. "I'm so glad you're the one my grandson married. He chose better than any of us realized."

Caroline's smile became a bit more natural. At least she had won one family member's approval. Together they watched as Luke's chest rose and fell in the quiet bedroom. Even the sound of the mantel clock's rhythmic ticking faded as the mint-scented steam filled the room.

Sleep overtook Caroline, and her head fell forward. The motion startled her back into wakefulness, and Caroline leaned forward in the rocker. Grandma Darby had also succumbed to exhaustion, her head resting against the back of her chair. Caroline debated whether or not to wake her but decided against it.

She stood and checked on her husband, laying her hand on his forehead. Was his skin cooler? She moved her hand to his chest. He was definitely cooler. Happiness flooded her. Caroline wanted to dance about the room. She wanted to shout the news from the rooftop. Luke was getting better.

She checked the teapot. With a lighter heart and a

renewed sense of purpose, she picked it up and took it downstairs to be refreshed. Luke was getting better.

⠶

"You look especially beautiful this morning. I love the way your dress brings out the blue of your eyes." Luke's admiring gaze set butterflies fluttering in Caroline's stomach.

She bustled about the bedroom, fluffing the pillows on Luke's bed and straightening the books on his bedside table. "Thank you, Luke. You are looking quite dashing yourself this morning."

Luke raked a hand through his dark hair. "I could use a haircut."

She stopped her nervous actions and took a moment to study him, trying to ignore how wonderful he looked sitting in the tall-backed chair next to the fireplace. "I don't know if you'll like the result, but I can try—"

"Oh no." He shook his head. "You may have faced down the Yankee army on my behalf and brought all of us safely to Shady Oaks, but I only trust Hezekiah's steady hand with the hair clippers."

Rolling her eyes, Caroline took the tray from his lap, checking to make certain he had eaten all his breakfast. She treasured the banter between them. It was only one of God's blessings that had come about as her husband recovered from his wounds. He had changed so much—the sometimes arrogant, always self assured man she had fallen in love with had softened. If only she could be confident that she was the woman he loved.

Several times over the past days his gaze had seemed to declare his love, but Luke remained mute on the subject. When she was with him in this room, all her fears and doubts seemed foolish, the imaginings of an overwrought mind. But the moment she left him to tend to her other duties, the specter of Amelia arose once more. And one question above all others came to the forefront of her erratic thoughts. Whom did he really love?

Why hadn't she told him yet that she was carrying their child? Was she scared of his reaction? Scared that he would express love for her only because of the baby?

At first she had convinced herself to remain silent so he could focus on his own health. As the days wore on, it seemed there were so many other things to talk about. Luke read his Bible daily, and they discussed the meaning of many scriptures. Even though she was a pastor's daughter, Caroline found herself challenged by Luke's insightful questions.

Earlier this week she had listened as he talked about his guilt over the death of his friend Hampton. She prayed with him for the men who fought on both sides of the war. They discussed heaven and the afterlife, the importance of spreading the Gospel and her family's ministry. Yesterday they had even made plans to visit her parents in Jackson and her grandparents in Natchez as soon as travel became safe again. But still she had not been able to tell him about the life growing inside her.

"After Hezekiah finishes, will you come down to the parlor today? It's a bit chilly this morning to sit outside, but Grandma Darby and I would love to have you join us in the front parlor while we work on the mending."

He nodded. "I think it's time for me to rejoin the world."

Caroline pondered her husband's statement as she carried Luke's tray downstairs and searched out Hezekiah. Was Luke referring to life on the plantation? Or did he think he needed to rejoin the Confederate army? She hoped he did not think he was strong enough to return to battle. She walked toward the parlor, smiling at Grandma Darby as she took her place on the sofa and picked up her needle.

"How is our patient today?"

"Stronger than ever. He should be down shortly."

"You've done such a good job caring for him, Caroline."

"We all do our parts, but it is God who deserves the praise. He has mended Luke and given him back to us."

The two of them worked in companionable silence, the only sound in the room the crackle of a cheerful fire that removed the spring chill from the air.

A sound at the door brought her head around. Fully dressed, Luke didn't much resemble the unkempt patient she had seen earlier. His face was brown in comparison to the frothy white cravat showing above the lapels of his blue frock coat. A part of her wished she could halt the forward march of time, even return to the days of Luke's convalescence. Guilt washed through her with the thought. It wasn't that she wished for Luke to be ill again, but she didn't want him to reassume the imperiousness that had made her feel so disconnected from him.

The sound of horses' hooves on the drive outside interrupted her train of thought and made Caroline's heart thump. Had the war come to them at Shady Oaks?

Luke frowned and disappeared into the hall, returning a few moments later with a folded sheet of vellum in one hand.

"What is it, Luke?" Grandma Darby asked the question uppermost in Caroline's mind.

Luke's face was drawn, paler than when he'd first come downstairs. "A soldier has brought me a note from Major Fontenot."

Caroline's heart clenched. "What news is so important it must be delivered by messenger?"

"They need me to return to Vicksburg."

"You can't go." Caroline couldn't stop the objections trembling on her tongue. "You're barely recovered."

"I cannot cower here when my strength and expertise might do some good." He picked up the sock she'd been mending and set it on the arm of the sofa before taking a seat next to her. "I hoped we would have more time together, but it seems that is not to be."

Caroline barely heard Grandma Darby make some excuse and leave them alone. Tears stung her eyes. This was a disaster. Would they never have time to mend their differences? And what about the baby? She had to tell him. It might not be enough to stop him from going, but perhaps it would give him a reason to look forward to returning. They needed to discuss so many things, but when? It seemed this was the only time they would have.

"Do you know how expressive your face is, Caroline?"

The look in his eyes made her heart beat faster. "Th–thank you."

He took her hand in his. "I sometimes forget how lovely you are."

Her gaze drank in every detail of him, from the soft, dark waves of his hair to the polished leather of his boots. "I'm not sure you're strong enough."

His endearing smile appeared, making her breath catch in her throat. Would she ever be able to control his effect on her?

"Yes I am, thanks to you and Grandma." He squeezed her hand before raising it to his lips.

Caroline's arms erupted in gooseflesh. "Hezekiah is the one who did the hardest work. I still marvel at the way he carried you to Vicksburg after you were shot."

"I freed him, you know, before he brought me back. Hezekiah will never have to answer to anyone except God for his decisions."

"I'm so glad."

His smile was warm. "That's only the first of the many improvements I intend to make upon my return."

"I can hardly wait." Her stomach shifted, prompting her to change the subject. "I have something important to tell you."

"Your confession is not important. Not until I tell you something very important."

Caroline's heart sped up. Was he about to declare his love? Why now? Why could he not have said something days earlier?

"I was teasing you earlier, but I want you to know how much I admire the bravery you showed while I was too sick to protect you and Grandma. I'm very proud of the way you stood up to an army of Yanks."

Blood rushed to her cheeks. Caroline tried to pull her hand free, but Luke kept it imprisoned. Where were the words of love she was expecting? "I don't deserve your esteem. I was nearly too frightened to get the first word out."

The whole world seemed to slide away as their glances met. She could not look away. She was lost in the depths of his dark gaze. Silence filled the room, and time ground to a halt.

"You are very courageous, my dear. One of God's many blessings in my life."

Caroline closed her eyes for a moment, a conflict raging inside her as violent as any battlefield. She wanted to revel in the happiness of this moment, but she could not. She might have his admiration now, but did Luke love her? Or was he still in love with the girl from Tennessee? The memory of his words the day he discovered her and Dinah returned, forming a wall between them.

She thought she'd buried her pain. Perhaps she had. . . and watered it, too. Because it had grown into a vine that threatened to strangle their marriage. This time he let her go when she pulled at her hands. Caroline stood and walked to the fireplace.

"What is it?" Luke pushed himself up and came to stand behind her.

Caroline stared blindly at the mantel. How could she think when all she wanted to do was turn around and hide her face against his strong chest? But if she continued to bury her true feelings, could their marriage survive?

After silently debating which course to take, Caroline turned and faced him. "I know I'm not the woman you truly love."

❧

His wife's expression was a mixture of pain and determination. Luke felt like she'd punched him in the stomach. Hadn't he just told her how much he admired her? But after a moment, he realized he needed to bare his past if he hoped to have a future with the woman standing in front of him. "You mean Amelia."

"And Marianna, too, for that matter."

He nodded. This was going to be hard, but it had to be done. He had to convince Caroline that he loved her and her only. He remembered the promise he'd made to God. He would do whatever he could to reassure her, to regain her love and respect. He was the one who needed to confess.

"Amelia Montgomery and I grew up together. Our parents always assumed we would one day marry, and I saw no reason to disagree. She had other ideas, however. I escorted her to Knoxville when her parents sent her to stay with relatives. While there, she got involved with the Underground Railroad and was eventually discovered. I thought my heart was broken by her deceit and her choosing someone else over me, and maybe it was."

A soft cry pulled Luke from the past. He looked down

at Caroline, surprised to see the sheen of tears brightening her eyes. Wishing he could submerge himself in the liquid blue, he sighed. "I suppose I was looking for someone more traditionally minded when I came down here to lick my wounds. So I focused on Marianna Lister." He could feel a smile turn up his lips. "I could never imagine someone like the proper Miss Lister getting involved in the Underground Railroad. She is consumed with more mundane concerns— the number of flounces on her skirt or the latest dance steps."

He sighed as he saw a tear spill over and roll down Caroline's cheek. "For a short while, I thought I could live with that, but then I met a golden-haired beauty who was neither too worldly nor too accomplished. A young woman with faith to inspire me to become a better man." Luke knelt in front of her and grasped both of Caroline's hands. "A woman whose quiet example has helped lead me into a closer relationship with Jesus."

Another tear followed the first down her cheek and landed on their clasped hands.

"Please don't cry, dearest. You have my heart. You have the best of both of the women I once considered. When I was lying in that cave, weak and wounded, I asked the Lord into my heart. He resides within me now, and I am no longer the man I once was. That's why I've been asking you so many questions lately about the scriptures. I feel such a need to understand, to absorb all of God's Word."

"That's wonderful, Luke. I guess I didn't realize how far you were from God."

"I was a fool. I thought I was in control of my life, but I have learned otherwise. I am learning to turn that control over to Him. I've read His Word all my life, but now the Bible is personal. Now I understand the sacrifice He made for me even though I was nothing but a worthless sinner. My eyes have been opened, and I can truly appreciate the woman I married."

Caroline sank to the floor in front of him. "I love you, Luke, with all of my heart. I'm sorry for questioning you."

"You had the right." He gathered her close. "I've been so wrong. Can you ever forgive me?"

"Of course I can. It makes it so much easier when I understand your past. Can you forgive me for being secretive?"

"Yes. I have come to realize your desire to help the slaves. I told Hezekiah that I plan to free all of our slaves and help them get started however we can. I trust my decision meets with your approval. . .?"

The light in her eyes was all the answer he needed. Luke leaned toward her, planning to taste the sweetness of her lips, but she ducked before he reached his goal. "What is it, dearest? Is something still bothering you?"

"N—no. Well. . .yes. As a matter of fact, I have some very special news. I've been waiting for what seems an eternity to tell you."

Another problem? He would not allow whatever was worrying her to come between them. "Whatever this problem is, Caroline, we will face it together."

A blush darkened her cheeks, increasing his curiosity. "I have been feeling a bit out of sorts for the past weeks—sick and irritable."

"I would never describe you as irritable, Caroline." He winked at her, hoping to ease her discomfort. "Not since you and Grandma ironed out your differences anyway."

She put a hand on his mouth. "Please don't distract me, Husband, or I will never manage to get to the point."

"All right. Tell me straight out. I'm completely recovered, and we don't have much time. If you're sick, I will make sure someone is here to nurse you as well as you have taken care of me. And when I get back, I'll put cotton in my ears if you're still irritable. That way I'll be spared your complaints."

She giggled. "I'm not sick, not really. It's just that. . . well. . .we're going to have an extra guest at Christmas this year."

He must be dense because he could not make sense of what she was trying to tell him.

Caroline sighed and leaned close enough that he could feel her breath on his cheek. "You're going to be a father."

The whispered words swirled around in his head, shocking him into absolute silence. A father? He was going to be a father? "You're expecting?" His voice broke on the last word. He grabbed her shoulders and pushed her back enough to see her face. The confirmation was there, along with her hesitant joy.

He pulled her close again and dropped quick kisses on her forehead and cheek before claiming her lips. They were going to have a child! What a miracle! She was so soft, so yielding—the mother of his children. Feeling her kiss him back was sweeter than anything he'd ever imagined. A prayer of thanks filled his heart and mind. Luke knew he would spend the rest of his life thanking God for all His blessings.

epilogue

July 21, 1863

A feeling of homesickness filled Caroline as she looked out over the front lawn. What would Ma and Tory be doing today? Were they okay? It was so hard being separated from them. Had her family escaped to Natchez? Or were they still in Jackson? How she wished for some news, but Shady Oaks was too remote. They were cut off from everyone.

Caroline turned from the window to face Grandma Darby, one hand absently rubbing her slightly rounded stomach. "I think I'll go outside to pick some flowers now that the rain has stopped. The arrangement in the entry hall is sorely in need of replacement."

"Don't wander far from the house, dear." The older woman flipped idly through the pages of a *Godey's Lady's Book* that had to be almost a year old. "The overseer said he saw some drifters yesterday down by the river."

"I won't. I just feel so out of sorts. And the baby has been restless all day long. Maybe a walk will do us both good." Caroline left the older woman, lifting her skirt to avoid a soaking as she headed for the garden shed for shears and a basket.

When she had the necessary implements for her task, Caroline walked to the flower garden and began gathering the fresh blossoms. Hot, golden sunshine poked through the fleeing storm clouds, raising steam from the damp grass and hedges. The air wrapped around her face like a warm sponge as she worked.

Soon her basket was full of fragrant flowers. Caroline straightened and turned to retrace her steps when her gaze fell on two bedraggled strangers walking toward Shady Oaks on the main drive. Her heart thumped unpleasantly. They had been so blessed to remain untouched by the battles waging in the state, and she prayed these men would not threaten their peace. Tales of burned-out homes and crops haunted her, but Caroline pushed them away as she moved to intercept the strangers.

The shade of the towering oaks lining the drive hid their features at their current distance, but she could tell that one of the men was limping. He was white, and his larger companion was a black man. The lame one turned his head to say something, and her breath caught.

She knew that profile. The basket of flowers fell at her feet. "Luke!" Joy replaced her fear as Caroline ran toward them. She reached him and threw her arms around her husband, almost knocking him down in her enthusiasm. "I'm so happy to see you." She tried to hide the catch of worry in her voice. He was thin, far thinner than he'd been when he left for Vicksburg. His uniform hung loose, as though it had been made to fit a giant.

"Until now I don't think I ever fully understood the meaning of the phrase 'You're a sight for sore eyes.'" Luke bent his head and covered her lips with his own.

She melted at the familiar touch, but their baby kicked out, apparently not as pleased by the embrace as his mother. Caroline's cheeks flushed.

Luke held her at arm's length, a look of shock on his face. Then he laughed and wrapped his arms around her more gingerly.

Caroline emerged from her husband's embrace and looked over his shoulder at Hezekiah. "Both of you look exhausted.

Let's get you inside. I know Dinah is going to be as excited as I am. I hope the two of you are ready to be pampered and coddled."

She placed her shoulder under her husband's arm to help steady him as they moved down the drive together. "Is it true Vicksburg has fallen to the Yankees?"

Luke nodded. "We held them off in pitched battles, but Grant's siege doomed us to failure. We could not get supplies past them, and we never received any reinforcements. Food disappeared within the first few weeks. People were reduced to eating horse meat and even rats at the end. And the daily barrage of cannon fire destroyed almost everything in the city. People dug tunnels or took shelter in caves along the riverbank."

Imagining the deprivation he had faced made Caroline feel ill. "Why didn't everyone escape down the river?"

"Where would they go? Every settlement from New Orleans to Memphis is under Federal control." He shook his head. "Vicksburg was the final town. General Pemberton's surrender gave the Yankees their final victory. They have a choke hold on the Confederacy. It's only a matter of time until the war will be over."

His words brought her hope. The war couldn't end soon enough for her. They climbed the steps slowly, and she pushed the front door open. "Look who has come home."

Her raised voice brought Grandma Darby to the entry hall as well as the household slaves. Soon they were in the midst of a crying, laughing, chattering group of people. After everyone had a chance to welcome the master home, Caroline sent Cora and her kitchen assistants out back to prepare a special meal to celebrate the heroes' return. The housekeeper, Mabel, shooed the maids upstairs to get the bedchamber refreshed. Dinah dragged Hezekiah outside to their cabin on the far side of the cane fields so she and their children could tend to him.

Luke escorted Grandma Darby to her chair before taking a seat next to Caroline in the parlor. "It's good to be home."

"Yes." Grandma Darby picked up the needlework she'd abandoned earlier. "We're relieved you're safe and sound."

"It's due to God lending us strength and endurance." Luke gazed out one of the windows, but Caroline had the feeling he was not seeing the front lawn. "If not for His faithfulness, we would have perished several times. Once Pemberton surrendered, we were all taken prisoner. Our weapons were confiscated, but we at least were given food to eat. It took some time, but most of my men were furloughed." He stopped for a moment, and his gaze refocused. He looked down at Caroline, his eyes sad. "The ones who didn't die in the siege, that is."

Caroline wished she could ease the pain in his expression. *Lord, please help me do the right thing for my husband.*

After a moment, Luke sighed and continued. "Hezekiah found me as soon as I was released, and we started for home. That was three days ago."

"Praise God." The heartfelt words came from Grandma Darby.

Caroline echoed her sentiment.

Luke shook himself and reached for Caroline's hand. "Enough about me. How are you feeling? How's the baby?"

"I feel wonderful now that you're here. And the baby must be healthy, judging by his activities day in and day out."

Luke put a gentle hand on her stomach. "It's a miracle I can't wait to see you holding our child in your arms."

A vision of the four of them took root in her mind—she and Grandma Darby nurturing the baby while Luke set the child's feet on the narrow path to deep and abiding faith. And God willing, they would have other children, children who would fill the halls of Shady Oaks with love and laughter. She leaned against the back of the sofa.

"Is something wrong, Caroline?" Luke's voice was filled with concern.

Caroline shook her head. "Everything is very right."

A rustle from the other side of the room indicated Grandma Darby's tactful exit.

Luke released her hand and took her in his arms. "I love you, Caroline. I thought of you so often while I was stuck in Vicksburg."

"I prayed for you every night, dearest."

"Your prayers kept me alive. I could feel God's touch even in the hardest days, even when men and women were dying around me." He feathered kisses on her cheeks and forehead before capturing her lips with his own.

Time stood still as they shared soft words of love and devotion. The war might not quite be over, but at Shady Oaks, peace beyond all understanding flowed strong and true.

A Letter To Our Readers

Dear Reader:

In order that we might better contribute to your reading enjoyment, we would appreciate your taking a few minutes to respond to the following questions. We welcome your comments and read each form and letter we receive. When completed, please return to the following:

Fiction Editor
Heartsong Presents
PO Box 719
Uhrichsville, Ohio 44683

1. Did you enjoy reading *As the River Drifts Away* by Diane T. Ashley and Aaron McCarver?
   ❏ Very much! I would like to see more books by this author!
   ❏ Moderately. I would have enjoyed it more if

   _____

   _____

   _____

2. Are you a member of **Heartsong Presents**? ❏ Yes ❏ No
   If no, where did you purchase this book? _____

   _____

3. How would you rate, on a scale from 1 (poor) to 5 (superior), the cover design? _____

4. On a scale from 1 (poor) to 10 (superior), please rate the following elements.

   ____ Heroine   ____ Plot
   ____ Hero   ____ Inspirational theme
   ____ Setting   ____ Secondary characters

5. These characters were special because? _____

_____

_____

6. How has this book inspired your life? _____

_____

_____

7. What settings would you like to see covered in future
   Heartsong Presents books? _____

_____

_____

8. What are some inspirational themes you would like to see
   treated in future books? _____

_____

_____

9. Would you be interested in reading other **Heartsong
   Presents** titles? ❑ Yes ❑ No

10. Please check your age range:
    ❑ Under 18   ❑ 18-24
    ❑ 25-34   ❑ 35-45
    ❑ 46-55   ❑ Over 55

Name _____

Occupation _____

Address _____

City, State, Zip _____

E-mail _____

IDAHO BRIDES

The three McConnell brothers
are each trying to overcome a
tainted childhood as a drunkard's
son. Can love bring each of them
the freedom they desire?

Historical, paperback, 352 pages, 5.1875" x 8"

Please send me ____ copies of *Idaho Brides*. I am enclosing $7.99 for each.
(Please add $4.00 to cover postage and handling per order. OH add 7% tax.
If outside the U.S. please call 740-922-7280 for shipping charges.)

Name _____

Address _____

City, State, Zip _____

To place a credit card order, call 1-740-922-7280.
Send to: Heartsong Presents Readers' Service, PO Box 721, Uhrichsville, OH 44683

Heartsong

Any 6 Heartsong Presents titles for only $20.95*

GET MORE FOR LESS FROM YOUR HISTORICAL ROMANCE!

Buy any assortment of six *Heartsong Presents* titles and save 25% off the already discounted price of $3.99 each!

*plus $4.00 shipping and handling per order and sales tax where applicable.
If outside the U.S. please call
740-922-7280 for shipping charges.

HEARTSONG PRESENTS TITLES AVAILABLE NOW:

___HP756 *The Lumberjack's Lady*, S. P. Davis
___HP767 *A Bride Idea*, Y. Lehman
___HP771 *Canteen Dreams*, C. Putman
___HP775 *Treasure in the Hills*, P. W. Dooly
___HP779 *Joanna's Adventure*, M. J. Conner
___HP780 *The Dreams of Hannah Williams*, L. Ford
___HP784 *Promises, Promises*, A. Miller
___HP787 *A Time to Laugh*, K. Hake
___HP788 *Uncertain Alliance*, M. Davis
___HP791 *Better Than Gold*, L. A. Eakes
___HP792 *Sweet Forever*, R. Cecil
___HP807 *The Greatest Find*, P. W. Dooly
___HP808 *The Long Road Home*, R. Druten
___HP815 *A Treasure Regained*, P. Griffin
___HP819 *Captive Dreams*, C. C. Putman
___HP820 *Carousel Dreams*, P. W. Dooly
___HP823 *Deceptive Promises*, A. Miller
___HP824 *Alias, Mary Smith*, R. Druten
___HP828 *A Season for Grace*, T. Bateman
___HP836 *A Love for Keeps*, J. L. Barton
___HP847 *A Girl Like That*, F. Devine
___HP848 *Remembrance*, J. Spaeth
___HP872 *Kind-Hearted Woman*, J. Spaeth
___HP887 *The Marriage Masquerade*, E. Vetsch
___HP888 *In Search of a Memory*, P. Griffin
___HP891 *Sugar and Spice*, F. Devine
___HP892 *The Mockingbird's Call*, D. Ashley and A. McCarver
___HP895 *The Ice Carnival*, J. Spaeth
___HP896 *A Promise Forged*, C. C. Putman
___HP899 *The Heiress*, L. A. Eakes
___HP900 *Clara and the Cowboy*, E. Vetsch

___HP903 *The Lightkeeper's Daughter*, P. W. Dooly
___HP904 *Romance Rides the Range*, C. Reece
___HP907 *The Engineered Engagement*, E. Vetsch
___HP908 *In Search of a Dream*, P. Griffin
___HP911 *The Prodigal Patriot*, D. Franklin
___HP912 *Promise of Tomorrow*, S. Moore
___HP915 *The Newcomer*, L.A. Eakes
___HP916 *Lily and the Lawman*, E. Vetsch
___HP919 *The Columns of Cottonwood*, S. Robbins
___HP920 *Across the Cotton Fields*, D. Ashley and A. McCarver
___HP923 *Romance Rides the River*, C. Reece
___HP924 *The Displaced Belle*, P. W. Dooly
___HP927 *In Search of Serenity*, P. Griffin
___HP928 *Maggie and the Maverick*, E. Vetsch
___HP931 *Bridge to Love*, D. Franklin
___HP932 *Promise of Yesterday*, S. Moore
___HP935 *Mutiny of the Heart*, V. McDonough
___HP936 *Leave Me Never*, C. Stevens
___HP939 *Romance at Rainbow's End*, C. Reece
___HP940 *Dinner at the St. James*, S. Robbins
___HP943 *Among the Magnolias*, D. Ashley & A. McCarver
___HP944 *The Reluctant Outlaw*, P. W. Dooly
___HP947 *Love's Raid*, D. Franklin
___HP948 *Promise of Time*, S. Moore
___HP951 *Revealing Fire*, C. Stevens
___HP952 *Before the Dawn*, E. Vetsch
___HP955 *White River Dreams*, F. Devine
___HP956 *I'd Sooner Have Love*, J. L. Barton
___HP959 *Blues Along the River*, S. Robbins
___HP960 *Yankee Heart*, J. A. Davids

(If ordering from this page, please remember to include it with the order form.)

Presents

Great Inspirational Romance
at a Great Price!

Heartsong Presents books are inspirational romances in
contemporary and historical settings, designed to give you
an enjoyable, spirit-lifting reading experience. You can
choose wonderfully written titles from some of today's
best authors like Wanda E. Brunstetter, Mary Connealy,
Susan Page Davis, Cathy Marie Hake, Joyce Livingston,
and many others.

When ordering quantities less than six, above titles are $3.99 each.
Not all titles may be available at time of order.

SEND TO: Heartsong Presents Readers' Service
P.O. Box 721, Uhrichsville, Ohio 44683
Please send me the items checked above. I am enclosing $ _____
(please add $4.00 to cover postage per order. OH add 7% tax. WA
add 8.5%). Send check or money order, no cash or C.O.D.s, please.
To place a credit card order, call 1-740 922-7280.

NAME _____

ADDRESS _____

CITY/STATE _____ ZIP_____

HPS 8-11

HEARTSONG PRESENTS

If you love Christian romance...

$12.99

You'll love Heartsong Presents' inspiring and faith-filled romances by today's very best Christian authors...Wanda E. Brunstetter, Mary Connealy, Susan Page Davis, Cathy Marie Hake, and Joyce Livingston, to mention a few!

When you join Heartsong Presents, you'll enjoy four brand-new, mass-market, 176-page books—two contemporary and two historical—that will build you up in your faith when you discover God's role in every relationship you read about!

Imagine...four new romances every four weeks—with men and women like you who long to meet the one God has chosen as the love of their lives...all for the low price of $12.99 postpaid.

Mass Market 176 Pages

To join, simply visit www.heartsong presents.com or complete the coupon below and mail it to the address provided.

YES! Sign me up for Heartsong!

NEW MEMBERSHIPS WILL BE SHIPPED IMMEDIATELY!
Send no money now. We'll bill you only $12.99 postpaid with your first shipment of four books. Or for faster action, call 1-740-922-7280.

NAME _____

ADDRESS_____

CITY_____ STATE _____ ZIP _____

MAIL TO: HEARTSONG PRESENTS, P.O. Box 721, Uhrichsville, Ohio 44683
or sign up at WWW.HEARTSONGPRESENTS.COM